OPPORTUNITY
KNOCKS

ALSO BY ALISON SWEENEY

The Star Attraction: A Novel

Scared Scriptless: A Novel

All the Days of My Life (So Far)

The Mommy Diet

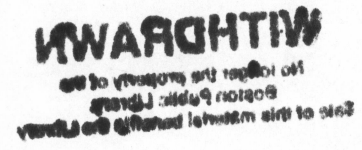

OPPORTUNITY KNOCKS

A NOVEL

ALISON SWEENEY

NEW YORK   BOSTON

Copyright © 2016 by Bookmark Entertainment Productions, Inc.
Cover design by Marlyn Dantes
Cover copyright © 2016 by Hachette Book Group, Inc.

Hachette Books
Hachette Book Group
1290 Avenue of the Americas
New York, NY 10104
HachetteBookGroup.com
twitter.com/hachettebooks

First Edition: April 2016

Hachette Books is a division of Hachette Book Group, Inc.
The Hachette Books name and logo are trademarks of Hachette Book Group, Inc.

The publisher is not responsible for websites (or their content) that are not owned by the publisher.

Library of Congress Cataloging-in-Publication Data

ISBN 978-0-316-26160-9 (Trade paperback ed.); ISBN 978-1-4789-0898-2 (Audiobook downloadable ed.); ISBN 978-0-316-26159-3 (Ebook ed.)

Names: Sweeney, Alison, 1976– author.
Title: Opportunity knocks : a novel / Alison Sweeney.
Description: First edition. | New York ; Boston : Hachette Books, 2016.
Identifiers: LCCN 2015044435| ISBN 978-0-316-26160-9 (paperback) | ISBN 978-1-4789-0898-2 (audio download) | ISBN 978-0-316-26159-3 (ebook)
Subjects: | BISAC: FICTION / Contemporary Women. | FICTION / Romance / Contemporary.
Classification: LCC PS3619.W4424 O67 2016 | DDC 813/.6—dc23 LC record available at http://lccn.loc.gov/2015044435

Printed in the United States of America

RRD-C

10 9 8 7 6 5 4 3 2 1

To my parents, who encouraged me to dream big, and then taught me to work hard to make those dreams come true.

OPPORTUNITY
KNOCKS

TO: Mom, Dad
FROM: A.Cleary.Makeup@mynet.net
SUBJECT: Mistakes
DATE: May 18, 2016

Dear Mom and Dad,

I'm so sorry I haven't emailed or called lately. At first everything was all so exciting and wonderful. I wanted to wait and surprise you with proof of how successful I could be out on my own. And then it all fell apart and I was too embarrassed to tell you. You both probably saw this coming from the beginning, but I didn't.

It's like a nightmare I can't wake up from. Where do I even begin to explain how something so wonderful turned into such a complete disaster? The bottom line is, my entire future is about to go down the drain. And that's not an exaggeration. I shouldn't even be spending the time typing this right now. I only have two days to prevent my career from completely crashing and burning. And unless you have an extra $5 million lying around that you never mentioned to me, I am in deep trouble. Can she send me to prison if I can't pay? I don't even know.

Mom, Dad, you have always been there for me. Sometimes that felt like too much. I wanted...no, I needed to get out on my own. But I didn't see the quicksand until I was stuck in it. Now everything's totally gone to hell and I have to find a way to get myself out of it. On my own. I mean, what's my choice? Even if you had that kind of money I am not going to bring you both down with me. No way. That's not how my story ends. I'm not sure what I'm going to do, but I'm going to figure out some way to fix this.

Love,
Alex

DELETE ALL? Um, yes. Stupid computer. Of course delete that pathetic, not to mention desperate, email. I am not a quitter. Now there *is* a plan. It may be outrageous and stupidly risky, but it can work. I'm not going to spend the rest of my life in debt to the devil.

CHAPTER ONE

∽

March

"You want me to put makeup on her *what*?" I press the phone tightly to my ear, convinced it must be a bad connection. "Who gets a tattoo there?" I mutter to myself after hanging up with today's boss. I like that every day is a new job, always something different...but there is a downside, too. Slipping my iPhone into my back pocket, I walk to where the "models" are waiting patiently for me to get to work.

I've only been a makeup artist for a year. And believe me, it's a lot harder than I thought it would be to get to the level where I'm doing touch-ups on Ryan Reynolds on the set of his latest action adventure. Honestly, if it weren't for the way my parents look at me every Sunday night at dinner, like this time they're sure I'll admit I can't hack it, I probably would have given up months ago. They probably have bets in for how long it will be before I ask for my full-time assistant job at the family company back.

"So what'd he say?" asks Bambie. That's not a joke. Her name is Bambie—and she has it tattooed on her inner wrist. If only she'd stopped inking herself after that.

"He said he needs all of your tattoos covered." I start digging into my special effects kit for the concealers I'll need. It's a complicated process. There are three different types of makeup I use to make sure the dark tattoo ink really disappears. Sometimes it's even a four-step process, depending on skin tone. In the beauty academy I attended last year, I aced this course. I practiced on the tattoo on my hip every night until I could do it in my sleep. It's a small butterfly, but the wings are quite dark so it takes several layers of makeup to smooth the whole thing out. The tattoo? I'm an idiot. I got that tattoo for the obvious reason: a brief high school rebellion.

"Why's it so pink? The camera's gonna see that, you know." Bambie interrupts my thoughts as I soften the edges of the reddish makeup that serves as the first step.

"I'm not done yet, Bambie." I move some of my equipment out of the way so she can brace one delicate, pedicured foot on the table. "This is actually gonna take a minute, so why don't you rest your leg...um...here." I would really like to block out the fact that I am applying makeup with a tiny sponge to this girl's perfectly waxed...you know what.

Yes. That's what I am *really* doing. Why? Because I didn't know when I accepted this job that I would be spending my Saturday morning doing makeup (and covering tattoos) for a bunch of...um...call girls. Can you put that on a résumé? How was I supposed to know that Lonely Nights was an escort service? I thought it was some indie band.

Bambie pops her gum again and opens up the issue of *Identity* magazine she had folded in the pocket of the makeup chair. I pull out the blending kit that will go on top of the reddish makeup to match her skin tone. There's no foundation that matches this outrageously tanned skin where a bikini bottom should be, so I feel a bit like a scientist mixing colors to blend. If only my parents could see me now.

Finally, I head to set with my model, who hasn't bothered to put on a cover-up of any variety. I never really considered myself a prude; I grew up in LA, for God's sake. But I can't help but start to feel a growing admiration for the casual, confident way Bambie strolls to her position on the low tree branch where the camera is pointing.

"Wow, Alex, you did a great job; you can't see a hint of color." The voice of the photographer, Chris, is a bit muffled as he says this while looking through the viewfinder. It seems fabulously ironic that Chris is openly gay. Not everyone on set is. I look around, noticing the way Chris's lighting assistant can't seem to get the whiteboard secured into the C-stand because he's staring at Bambie slowly positioning herself to straddle the thick tree branch. I poke Chris in the side and toss my head toward the gawking twenty-year-old.

"Bradley!" Chris barks. Bradley startles and drops both the big white square of cardboard and the metal stand he's supposed to be securing it to.

"Sorry, Chris. It was just stuck for a second." Bradley quickly moves to fix his equipment, and even though I am still super uncomfortable about the whole situation, his preoccupation with the naked woman makes me snicker.

"Nice assistant, Chris. Where'd you find that kid? Your old high school?"

"Watch it, Alex...I rescued you from a wedding today, didn't I?"

"Yeah...you didn't exactly mention we were going to be doing a calendar shoot for the Best Little Whorehouse in Ventura, though, did you?" I whisper as discreetly as possible.

Chris snaps a test shot and moves to let me lean in and examine the image.

"Whorehouse? Is that even still what you call them?" Chris teases under his breath. We already act like old friends, even though we've really only bonded since I responded to the ad he posted at my beauty school ten months ago.

"Who cares what they call it? The point is, I thought

I was finally going to have something I could use for my website." I take liberties with his camera, zooming in to double-check my work—I make a mental note to pump up the color of her cheeks. When I scroll down to check my tattoo cover-up, I try to maintain a professional eye, acknowledging that the lighting hasn't affected the final result. It disappears into the rest of Bambie's skin tone.

"Man, I won't have to Photoshop...it...at all. You do nice work, Alex." Chris squints at my "work" briefly before resetting the lens to the original shot.

"Thanks." I can't help but feel flattered. Even if doing the makeup for this calendar shoot won't add to my credibility or give me a tear sheet I can use on my website, it's still a job. And any chance to practice my makeup skills is a good day. Chris is the best photographer I've worked with so far, and I'm glad to have him as a friend.

I pull a brush and a rosy pink cheek color (coincidentally called Orgasm) from my set bag and add some color to Bambie's cheeks before tucking myself behind the lighting equipment to watch Chris do his thing.

Bambie flips her hair around and arches her back, changing her pose for every shot. It's impressive—no way could I do that. Even with clothes on, I am just not meant to be on camera. I hate hearing the click of the camera taking a shot when I'm on set, even though it's just the photographer testing the lighting. At five foot five, I have a pretty good idea that my gypsy skirt and loose blouse don't make the most figure-flattering outfit I could have assembled. I can't help it—I'm a bit of a hippie, even by LA standards. I wear flip-flops every day, and usually a brightly patterned, cheerfully loose outfit. Everyone gives me gift certificates to Anthropologie for Christmas, which about sums up my style.

"Beautiful, Bambie. Keep it up, tilt your head up a little, find that light, honey. Yup. Just like that." Chris keeps up a steady dialogue with his models, and I can see how well they react to his direction. He's going to make it big someday.

With everything in Chris's and Bambie's hands now, I check my phone, killing time until Chris needs me to step in again. My straw-colored hair refuses to stay tucked neatly behind my ears, falling forward far enough to brush the screen. I can't help but notice the split ends. I need to get one of my classmates from beauty school to "practice" a haircut on me soon.

A few texts are waiting for me.

Emma: You're doing makeup for WHO? WHAT??
Are you teasing me? That can't be real!

Emma is my best friend. We met during our freshman year of high school and hit it off immediately. I am proud to say that while I was a popular girl in my class—captain of the cheerleading squad, thank you very much—I wasn't a bully. I used my powers for good. I welcomed Emma, a New York transfer, into our clique with the simple announcement that she was "cool beans." And that was that. We hung out the whole year, a small posse moving from class to class. It wasn't until she broke my heart by moving back to Manhattan the next summer that we became really tight. Even though our friendship has mostly transpired via email and text, she's my closest ally, the person who knows all my secrets, and the only one I trust enough to tell where I am really working today. Because for all the crap we give each other, I know she won't make fun of me for this or hold it against me as yet another reason why trying to build a career as a makeup artist is a bad idea.

Me: for REALS!!!!

I surreptitiously hold my phone to take a picture of the setup and add it to my text for Emma. You're not supposed to take pictures of the shoots you work on, due to secrecy and whatnot, but I know I can trust her to keep it to herself. I can't help but giggle knowing Emma is so uptight, she wouldn't show it to anyone even if she wanted to. In fact, it somehow makes the whole nutso experience worth it, knowing I'm probably making ultra-old-fashioned Emma squirm in her buttoned-up polo shirt.

While I wait for the photo to send, I keep going through my texts.

> Sean: How late do you think you're working tonight?
> We have dinner with your parents, don't forget.

Sean is my boyfriend. We've been dating on and off since junior year of high school. He started working for my parents that summer. I met him while he was on one of their crews building a pool at this fancy house in Encino. That's what my parents do. They have a construction company appropriately named Pool Paradise and they build really high-end, expensive pools and patios in LA. Well, mostly in the Valley, but still...they are really nice homes.

Now, Sean has been promoted all the way to a project manager. He's even designed a few layouts. My dad definitely sees him as his successor to running the business.

> Me: I didn't know we were eating with them tonight?
> I thought it was just you and me.

I'm only twenty-five and I'm definitely not thinking about getting married yet. I mean, yes, it's hard not to feel sappy and romantic with all the brides I've been doing makeup for lately. I have a deal with a local wedding coordinator to do the bride, all the bridesmaids, and usually the mother of the bride, too. It's a package deal with a hairdresser she knows. But that's really the only time weddings are on my mind. I'm starting to build a nice savings account so I can get out of my parents' house. That's goal numero uno.

A quick glance at Bambie confirms that she is still looking fabulous and Chris is still snapping away—I can't imagine what it was like when photographers had to waste time changing rolls of film. And not knowing what the photos look like until you print them out seems insane. Now there's a crowd of people approving images in front of a computer screen while we're still shooting. I return to my phone to see an instant reply from Sean.

Sean: I promised them we'd join them tonight. Don't you remember? I know I told you last night.
Me: No. I don't remember. I have dinner with my parents almost every night.
Sean: Sorry, A. You know how your dad can be, he was totally angling for us to be there, I couldn't say no.

Staring at his text, I know it's not fair to be upset. Even though my parents treat him like family, Sean's admitted to me that he always feels he has to impress them. He works six days a week for them, and busts his butt doing overtime he doesn't bill them for. One time, in a fight, I accused Sean of dating me to get in good with my parents. He was so offended and shocked I knew immediately I had been way off base. So maybe it's not on purpose, but I do think sometimes he kinda lumps me and my family together as a package deal. His family is all spread out and he never talks to his siblings. Sean loves our big family dinners, and I can't blame him; we come across like a pretty cool gang. So I decide to wait a second before I reply.

Before I can scroll down to the next unread text, Chris shouts my name. I tuck my phone in my bag and hurry over to where he's standing next to Bambie.

"Her lips are smudging. Can you fix it?" I look at her bright red lipstick while I pull out Q-tips and makeup remover from my set bag. With Chris hovering over my shoulder, I trace a path around the outside of Bambie's naturally lush lips. It's impossible not to compare them to my own decidedly narrower ones. I clean up the line, so there's again a clear definition between the berry red color I chose and her tan skin. I stuff the stained Q-tips back in my bag to toss out later. I reapply the lipstick with a brush to darken the color in the center without messing up the shape I just perfected.

"Don't smush," I instruct quickly. Meaning don't mash your lips together, something that most women do instinctively every time they put on lipstick or gloss. Normally it's not that big a deal, but the bright red color I used will really stain the skin around her lips if she mashes them too hard. Based on the murmuring around the computer screen, which is zoomed in to an ultra-close-up of Bambie's lips, and Chris breathing down my neck, I can't afford to let Bambie mess up my work.

"We good?" he asks as I swipe some loose powder across her forehead. "We've got eleven more months to get through before we lose the light." Luckily Bambie is good at taking orders. She freezes her face for a second, clearly still fighting to not rub her lips together, and then shoots me a smile before she stretches back out like a cat making the tree branch her home. I clear off the set, and Chris gets back to shooting.

I decide there's no point in running through the tried-and-true excuses I could use to get out of dinner with my parents tonight. I'm just going to have to suck it up. But I can't help thinking I'd rather cover up tattoos on a hundred girls than hear another lecture from my mom and dad.

CHAPTER TWO

⌒

"Shut up!" I dig my heel into Mark's foot under the table. For once, I wish I wore high-heeled shoes. Havaianas just don't have enough impact when trying to inflict pain on my older brother. Well, older by like five minutes. It was Mark, then me, then Juliet, who is the baby of the family, even though she was only two minutes behind me. Yup, my mom gave birth to triplets. Not to mention our two older brothers, Sam and Brett, who aren't here. Sam is a biotech professor at MIT. I pretty much haven't understood anything he's said since he got into high school. And Brett is currently serving in Southeast Asia. He's a pilot for the navy, something he wanted to do since he saw his first airplane.

"You shut up!" Mark retorts louder, making everyone at the table, including Sean, roll their eyes at us. For some reason Mark and I can never be in the same room without regressing to ten-year-old behavior.

I shoot Sean a look out of the corner of my eye. It's his

fault we're here, I remind him silently. If it were up to me we'd be on a nice quiet date, just the two of us. Hell, going to the Mexican restaurant down the street from my parents' house would be more peaceful than this. But Sean chooses to ignore my mental daggers and returns to a conversation with my mom about the latest project they're working on.

"How did the Melkans feel about our proposed location for the hot tub?" Sean asks as I try not to cringe with flashbacks to my day and the graphic hot tub images I hope will eventually fade from my mind.

"They loved your suggestion, Sean. It's the perfect solution. You and Mark should get started on it right away, though. I don't want it to slow down the delivery date, and we're already well into the pool excavation."

"Don't worry, Mom." Mark stops trying to tug the chipped pasta bowl out of my hands before I'm finished scooping out my portion. "Sean and I went over the deets yesterday."

"I'm going to bring on two extra crew Monday so we catch up to the pool, Winnie." Sean finishes off Mark's thought. I tune out the family business talk, focusing on my mom's favorite group meal—pasta with veggies.

"Delish, Mom," I say between bites, in case it's obvious I'm chowing down to facilitate a quick getaway.

"Thanks for saying so, princess." My mom smiles at me warmly. "I worry about you, off in those remote locations." In my mom's mind, when I'm working in the family office, I'm safe. Out on my own? Who knows what could happen? She doesn't say it out loud, but that is what she means.

"Yes, Winnie, it's great," Sean says, diverting me from getting into the familiar family conflict. I meet his eyes to thank him. I've resigned myself to the fact that my parents will never stop being overprotective of me. But some days it still gets under my skin.

They love me, but they trust Sean. He runs their business while I file papers on Fridays. If it were up to Mom and Pop, I would work for them forever. And before beauty school, I might have settled for that, too. But I've finally found a career; doing makeup is exactly right for me. Now I just have to prove I can make a living at it.

"Perfect-o, Mom." Mark does a fake Italian accent and kisses his fingers. Mark works at Pool Paradise, too. My dad runs the business end so that Mark and my mom can focus on designing the layouts. Did I mention Mark's an architect? As if I needed another sibling to show me up. Between my heroic oldest brother and Sam, it's already a tough household to get a word in edgewise.

So, my parents had Brett, then Sam, then decided they wanted to try for a girl. Since my mom was a little bit older at that point, it took some help from the modern technology of the nineties, and what do you know? She got pregnant with triplets. At least she got the girl she wanted.

Well, two of us, actually. My sister isn't here, either. She would totally gang up with Mark against me, which is one reason why I'm glad she's not. Another reason is that Juliet works for Teach For America. She sends me these incredible daily email updates about the really dangerous neighborhood in West Texas where she's teaching high school students how to read. She says it's her calling.

My point is, every one of my siblings has known what they wanted out of life since birth. Somehow that family tradition of drive and ambition skipped right over me. It's like the chicken or the egg—I don't know if they babied me because I didn't know what I wanted to do with my life, or if because I was so babied, I never figured out what I needed to do with my life.

"Hey, Al. Quit daydreaming and pass the wine." I instinctively dodge Mark's elbow and try to smack him in retaliation. He is equally quick in avoiding me.

"Children, enough. No wine for either of you if you can't act like adults." My father is a practical disciplinarian. Just like the threat of taking away my nail polish kit worked when I was twelve, the threat of having to go through the rest of this dinner without a fabulous Santa Ynez syrah—my parents always splurge on good wine—finally settles both Mark and me into adult behavior.

With one last severe look, my dad seems satisfied with our silence and passes the wine. Sean stifles a chuckle as he hands me the bottle and I refill my glass before maturely passing it to Mark.

"So, Alex, how did your photo shoot go today? You said it was for a wall calendar?"

I try not to choke on my wine. I consider myself a pretty cool, modern chick, but talking to my mom about the type of calendar I did today is just way outside my comfort zone.

"Who makes wall calendars anymore, anyway?" Leave it to Mark to zero in on the heart of the matter.

"That's a good point. Other than...um..." Sean hesitates over how to describe it... "*Sports Illustrated,*" he recovers smoothly, "who's making calendars?"

"Lots of people." I'm finding it impossible not to sound defensive. "I think they were building up Web content for their company, too." I search for innocuous details I can share. "We were shooting out at a ranch in Agoura Hills. There were horses and stuff. It was really pretty. But super hot. I kept having to touch up the models; they were sweating just sitting still." There. That feels like a safe enough amount of information.

"I hope you kept your water bottle with you. Heat is one of your triggers." My mom reaches over to pat my hand, and then quickly changes the subject before I can remind her I'm actually a grown woman. "Remember that pool we did for that musician in Agoura, Greg?" My mom turns her attention to my father, and they both chuckle. I polish off the last of my wine to keep from interrupting to defend myself with the fact that I haven't had an attack in months, but since Sean is already refilling my glass and Mark is carrying on about a new building going up downtown, it seems wiser to just let it go.

CHAPTER THREE

᠌⁓

Why, why, *why*? Normally the fact that the San Fernando Valley is consistently ten degrees—if not more—warmer than anywhere else in LA is one of my favorite things about it. I love being warm, as demonstrated by my closet, full of skirts and shorts and a colorful pile of sandals. But today, we've got to be well over one hundred degrees. And it's March. And I had to interrupt the photographer at least a dozen times already to touch up the clown makeup on the model.

Obviously, it was not *my* idea to do clown makeup on this guy. I was just hired to do a job, and for once, I might get a pretty cool image to add to my website, if the model stops dripping sweat through his white foundation. My phone pings as I step away back into the tiny patch of shade I've found.

Emma: Wow! That clown looks so sad.

I sent Emma the pic I took right when I finished his makeup. Before this heat wave melted my artwork.

Me: he's supposed to look sad. It's art. Lol.

Emma: Where did you find this photographer again? What kind of twisted childhood is he making up for?

Me: it's a she. The photog is a chick. I think—it's hard to tell through the black camo gear.

Emma: Lol.

Me: seriously...she has vision. We're in this alley with chain-link fence, beat-up cars on blocks, and graffiti on this really cool yellow garage door.

Emma: That sounds—really cool?

Me: yeah, it'd b cool—if it weren't so hot 2day! over 100. clown is sweating all over the place. It's so gross, & impossible to take more than 3 pics in a row w/o having 2 fix something.

Emma: I wish I could send you some of our cold.

Me: send me a pic of your freezer! bet your show has a freezer full of goodies. homemade popsicles?

Emma: You know I'm not allowed to take any behind-the-scenes pictures. :-/ And besides, I'm already layered up like the kid from A Christmas Story for my run around the reservoir today.

Me: work out for me. XO

Emma: XO

I put my phone away just in time for J—that's what the photographer goes by, just J—to glance my way.

"Hey, Alex. A little help on the right side. His teardrop is starting to smear." I rush in to touch it up, but when I look closely, the sweat has created a perfect black streak down his face from where I painted in the tear.

"J, what do you think? This actually looks really cool to me." I tilt the model's face for J to zoom in with her camera.

"I like it. We'll do a few like this," she says decisively. I leave the smudge, and instead of removing the sweat marks, I add a few more. So he looks like it's a stress issue rather than overheating.

"What if he's holding the coat over his shoulder, J? So you can see his white shirt is so sweaty? I mean, really... embrace it?" I walk back behind the lens. J pulls her pierced face away from the eyepiece of her fancy camera to size me up. It is a bit risky—I mean, this is her vision and she just hired me to help carry it out. "If you hate it, I can clean him all up in ten minutes," I quickly promise. J gestures for the hapless would-be clown to strip off the thick wool coat he's been suffering in. He swings it over his shoulder and all of a sudden the visual goes from cool and interesting to really edgy and intriguing. The white shirt is practically see-through in some places from sweat. And when he leans back into the chain-link fence with the colorful garage in the background, his face totally pulls focus, even on the mini viewfinder. This is a low-budget passion project for J, so she didn't spring to have the Mac on hand to review the images.

I can tell J loves how it looks now. She keeps snapping away; the shutter speed can hardly keep up with her. She hunches down and then goes up on her tiptoes, playing with camera angles, barking out orders for the model to change poses as she rotates around him.

When she's finally exhausted every possible combination, she comes back to where I'm standing, camera hanging around her neck. She pulls out a cigarette and sighs like she's just had the best sex of her life.

"That was a genius move, Alex. You have a good eye."

"Thanks, J." It is a super-rewarding feeling to know I helped make her vision a success. "You'll send me a jpeg I can use for my site? This will make an amazing image for my home page." And given that I took the job for fifty dollars, the jpeg is really the prize here. I'm desperate for content on my site; I know I won't ever get legit work if I don't have real photos, *professional* photos, on my page to show what I can do.

"Yeah, sure. I'll get it to you by the weekend. And I'm definitely going to call you again. You do beauty makeup too, right?" Before I can answer she goes on, not even looking at me now; she's scrolling back through the images on her camera's viewfinder. "I have a real job next week. I'll try to get you on it with me. That's more traditional stuff, you know, a catalog job." Thank God she can't see me practically foaming at the mouth. She says "catalog job" like it is poison, but to me it sounds like heaven. If I can get actual jobs that pay real money, I can move out of my childhood bedroom, which still has paint chips missing from the infamous *Lost* Poster Incident. How was I to know that the tape keeping Matthew Fox over my bed would ruin the faux paint scheme? I was thirteen. Yeah, moving out, that's definitely step one in proving to my parents I've finally got my act together.

CHAPTER FOUR

Emma is coming to visit this weekend! Well, she's coming here for work, but still, we'll get to hang out. We've been planning it for months, since the daytime TV show she works on announced they would be shooting on location in LA, but it always seemed so far away. And now, knowing I'll see my best friend tomorrow totally makes my day. Which I need, because every other thought in my head involves wanting to stab my eyes out. Doing the filing at the Pool Paradise office is by far the worst part of my week. But every Friday, unless I can actually justify skipping it with a legitimate makeup job, I have to drag myself into my parents' office in "appropriate business attire" and answer phones all day. My gladiator-style sandals are the nicest pair I own. They are a simple white, which matches my flowy white blouse. I put a white tank on underneath so no one would have an excuse to comment on how tissue-paper-thin the fabric is. It's hard to tell what my mom will consider "fancy" versus "inappropriate."

"Pool Paradise, may I help you?" I flick the computer screen away from one of the beauty blogs I follow, back to the company website.

"Hey, babe. It's me."

"Oh, thank God. Sean. I don't know if I can make it until lunch. You have to come rescue me." He chuckles at my dramatic desperation. Sitting behind a desk is killing my creative spirit.

"Somehow I knew you were going to say that. I was going to suggest you bring down the payroll so I can give the paychecks to the crew this afternoon. You could swing by and grab lunch..."

"Yes! I'll do it!" I don't even let him finish. Whatever it is that gets me out of here, I'm in. And of course, the fact that Sean is asking lends legitimacy to the request. If it were my idea, my dad would roll his eyes and remind me of my deal with my parents to work "just one day a week"—the implication being that's not asking too much—in exchange for living at home again.

"Dad! Where's the crew paychecks?" I holler into the narrow back office area. "Sean wants me to bring them out to the site."

"I haven't done them yet," he yells back.

"When will they be ready? He asked me to bring him some lunch so he can work straight through." Stretching my legs, I go to stand in his office doorway. If I keep my body open to the main area, my dad's closed-in lit-tle office space won't affect me. But I take evenly timed breaths just in case. "He says he thinks he's going to be able to wrap this job up by next week. So we can put both crews on the Melkans."

"Honey, I'll bring them out to you." He gestures me away from his door before his eyes return to the com-puter screen. I immediately breathe easier back in the wide-open front area. Dad raises his voice so I hear, "I can get it done in the next hour, before I head out to bid on a new job." I'll take that as a yes.

Knowing it's only an hour until freedom, I'm actually motivated to get some work done. I organize the bills and fill out some paperwork my dad left on my desk to get done today. It's not that I can't do this kind of work. I do oddly have a knack for math and numbers. I just loathe it.

I've been tough for my parents to deal with, but I couldn't help being a late bloomer. My dad will for-ever see me as the little girl whom he couldn't help. The agonizing minutes before the firemen came to get me out probably traumatized him more than me. My occa-sional bouts of claustrophobia certainly haven't helped either of us get past it. I love him for wanting to take care of me, but it's also restricting that they keep try-ing to mold me into what they want me to be instead of seeing that I've finally figured my life out. Makeup really is a dream come true for me. I love it, and am not going to give up on it just because it's tough breaking into the industry. I believe in myself, for once. It's just going to take time for me to prove it to everyone else.

"Here you go, sweetheart." I look up from the online billing program my parents are switching over to—way to join the twenty-first century, Pops—and see my dad extending a stack of envelopes toward me.

"Thanks, Dad. I'll be back by two."

"Sounds good. Don't forget to lock up; your mother isn't coming in today." And with that he's out the door. It takes me another twenty minutes to finish up my work. I may hate it, but I'm not irresponsible. Finally, I make my escape.

"TEN DOUBLE-DOUBLES. With onions. Can you make one of them protein style?" In the turnaround waiting to pull up to the cashier window, I update my Instagram account with a cool angle of the In-N-Out sign and the bright blue skies behind it.

Me: on my way with burgers.
Sean: sounds great. don't eat all the fries before you get here.
Me: omg...I only did that ONE time!
Sean: And stop TEXTING! You're driving!!

Me: Not driving yet. Eating your fries in the parking lot.

:) jk

Sean: you got me. Lol. See you soon.

I wipe my greasy fingers on my dark jeans—the ones with no rips in them—and roll up the paper bag so I'm not tempted to keep snacking on those damn delicious fries on the way to the work site.

The GPS on my phone—my bare-bones preowned Prius didn't come with any cool technology—leads me to a gorgeous Mediterranean-style home in Encino, south of Ventura Boulevard. The side gate is open as I find a place to park on the gorgeous pepper tree–lined street. I follow the sound of eighties rock music to the backyard, where the Paradise Pool crew is hard at work. Today they're laying in the steel rebar grid. There's steel mesh in stacks near the edge of the pool, which will be layered in this afternoon. The second my big white paper bags of Double-Doubles are in view, everyone drops what they're doing.

"Just in time, babe. We were starting to decide who we were going to sacrifice first."

"Glad I got here before that vote took place." Sean pulls my protein-style burger out of the bag and looks at the big lettuce leaves like they're snakes that might bite him. I take it from him before he drops it.

"What's wrong with a bun?"

"You know I'm trying to cut back on gluten."

"Really? Isn't that what pasta is? Gluten?"

Of course, I am fully equipped to retaliate equally passive-aggressively. "Don't you mean 'Thank you so much, Alex. You probably waited in the longest line ever at In-N-Out. I really appreciate it'?" I mimic his low voice and then, switching to an exaggerated falsetto version of myself, add, "Oh, you're welcome, sweetie! I'm happy to do it!"

"Okay, okay. Thank you for the burgers." He takes a big bite of one, but still manages to add while chewing, "Even though I know you did it just to get away from the office."

It seems a good idea to drop the subject, so I take a bite and enjoy every drop of special sauce as it's oozing onto my fingers.

"So what do you want to do this weekend?" There is a nonexistent pause that leaves no time for my input before he continues. "Let's go down to the beach again tomorrow—a bunch of guys want to play volleyball." Sean wolfs down the rest of his burger and licks his fingers. "You could be our cheerleader." He runs his hand along my thigh.

"I can't." I never thought I'd look forward to doing a wedding. But spending the day making sure "the guys" have ice-cold Coronas on hand isn't the fun day at the beach I once thought it would be. "I have a wedding tomorrow, remember?"

He gives me this puppy-dog look with his big brown eyes while polishing off some fries. I snatch a few from his basket and can't help but laugh at his cute face. "I could come afterward? We'll meet for drinks at that bar by the courts?"

"I knew you'd come." He leans forward to kiss me sweetly. We're both aware of the crew laughing and smoking nearby.

"I could take Uber so we can drive home together." And then, super casually, I add, "And stay over at your place after." With our faces still so close together, I can't help but sense him hesitate for a split second.

"Yeah, sure, babe. Sounds perfect." He kisses me again on the lips and then makes a big production of stuffing our trash back in his to-go bag and checking his diver's watch. Watching him practically lurch away from me, I bite my tongue to avoid saying something pathetic or needy.

We were together in high school. When he left for college, we took a break. But we easily fell into our old "together" routine when he came home, as if no time had passed. For almost five years now we've been exclusive. And just once, I'd love for him to pull some sexy man stuff. Instead I sometimes feel like we're still in this teenage "going steady" phase. I'm not saying I want *Fifty Shades of Grey* or anything, but something that puts a spark in my belly would be nice.

Leaning back against a tree to watch for a second as

Sean and the guys start gearing up to get back to work, it's easy to notice how good he looks in those jeans. His short, spiky dark hair is thick enough that I can run my fingers through it. And he's tall enough that even when I wore heels to my parents' anniversary party, I still tucked under his chin perfectly when we danced. I love how he gets along so well with my family. My parents obviously trust him; they've made it clear that Sean is going to run the company with Mark when they finally decide to retire. My brothers don't even give me a hard time about him. Sean and I fit together so well.

CHAPTER FIVE

Emma's text has gotten my butt in gear. I've spent my entire Saturday morning being completely lazy. My parents buy oranges early at the farmers market on Saturdays, and my dad squeezes fresh OJ for everyone. When we were kids that job was a lot more labor-intensive. Now it's just my parents and me in the house, so it's a smaller production. It is a really nice way to start the day. I considered spending some time cleaning out my bedroom, but I gave up when it came time to actually put Hello Kitty in the attic, so now I'm looking online at how to design my website. I have a few photos J left in Dropbox to get it started. I ran off a couple of sample business cards on my dad's laser printer. It took me several hours on Photoshop to decide exactly how I wanted them to look.

But now, I'm standing in the middle of reason 230 why I need to move out of my parents' house. I need more space than this tiny teenage bedroom full of high school memorabilia for my makeup kit. There's all this fancy special effects stuff I used in cosmetics school that I don't need on a daily basis. But I have to have it on hand, in case that kind of job comes along.

I was ignoring the mess around me that would get me cast on *Hoarders* in a second, and decided to focus on emailing a Web designer whose ad I liked on Facebook when Emma's text popped up on my phone. So now all my supplies are spread out all over the floor of my room, which has me freaking out trying to get ready. Luckily I've just done laundry. I may be freeloading off my parents, but my mom is not spending time separating my whites. It's a minor technicality, but an important separation of church and state as my mother continues to try to baby me. I can't even sit down right now because I have all my clean clothes in two big heaps on my queen-sized canopy bed, with original flower-patterned fabric hangings still intact.

Me: so excited for you to meet Emma tonight. She just texted me that she's here. Are you still ready to come get me around 5:15? Told Em we'd be there at 6.
Sean: crap…I forgot about that.
Me: u flaking?
Sean: I just got invited to the Lakers tonight. I mean, I'm sure someone'll want my tix—but wouldn't you rather have a night with your gf anyway? She's here all week right?

Me: yes. It's fine—go to your game. Just, promise
you'll see her this week.
Sean: promise. Thx babe.

Sean would be a total basket case if I forced him to
meet up with my friend instead of attending his beloved
Lakers game. My dad is a die-hard Dodgers fan, and has
taught me to love baseball and appreciate sports fanatics
in general, so I get it.

I pull a purple ombré gypsy skirt and a plain white
T-shirt out of my clean clothes pile. Throwing a couple
of long necklaces on, I find my purple Havaianas (under
the bed). Glancing at the Hello Kitty clock—that needs
to go to the attic, too—I transfer my wallet and mini
makeup bag to the matching hobo bag from the collec-
tion hanging on my bedpost and am ready to go.

It's been so long since I've seen Emma in person. I'm
both nervous and excited driving the 405 toward Santa
Monica, and I almost miss the interchange to the 10.

Emma is standing near the restaurant valet. Even
from a distance I can see her, standing out like the New
Yorker she is among the tourists and beachgoers hanging
around. I wave frantically to get her attention.

"Emma!" She spots me right away and strides over to
the car, sliding in smoothly.

"It's so good to see you!" Emma doesn't slow down
her momentum. She makes getting into the car and

leaning over to hug me all one movement. I squeeze her back.

"I missed you, too."

WE'VE BEEN HOLED up at this cool gastropub sharing sliders and truffle fries for hours. We text every day, but it's different, better, sharing the stories in person. My stomach hurts from laughing so hard.

"Well, I made up business cards online; they look pretty good too, I think." I pull one out of my wallet to show to her. I zoomed in on a close-up of a woman's eyes done with super-dramatic makeup.

"You did this? It's spectacular." I love how she's really checking out the details.

"She's one of the models from that, uh . . . you know, the calendar shoot I did?" Emma snorts a bit at the reminder. "Seriously, it was really cool she let me do this during her break, and I took a couple of pictures on my iPhone. You think it's good enough to use as the main image?"

"Oh, yeah, Alex. This is rad," Emma gushes.

"She had the coolest-shaped eyes."

"I bet she hears that all the time," Emma replies, sending us both into another fit of giggles.

It takes us a couple of minutes longer than it should to recover. The waiter comes over to check on us. "So, what are you gonna do with the cards?" Emma asks once he leaves. She's still slightly out of breath.

"I guess hand them out to photographers and publicists, people like that. J, that photographer I've done a few more shoots with? I told you about her, right? Supercool, kinda butch chick who is totally obsessed with clowns and circus stuff?"

"Does she do any normal work? That's what you need for your book, right?"

"Yeah, she did this Hollister campaign; there was already a lead makeup artist on the job, but I got to help her and she seemed really impressed. She's the one who recommended I make cards." I pull out my phone to show her some photos from the beach shoot.

"Why didn't you post these? They are amazing."

"This type of job is all top secret. You sign a waiver saying you won't Instagram or post any pictures from the shoot. I wasn't really supposed to take them, but I don't have a lot of pictures of my natural beauty makeup, so I at least want to have it on my phone."

"Well, you do love to defy authority, but you're so talented, no one will care. It's all going to come together. I can tell." She raises her refreshed wineglass to toast with my designated-driver-approved Coke Zero.

"I can't wait to see you work tomorrow, Em. I DVR the show just to see all the gorgeous food you make."

"I can't really take credit. I just follow the recipes."

"Are they really all her recipes?" I whisper.

"You know I can't talk about that stuff. Confidentiality," she scolds me.

"You're still such a rule follower. Ugh, how are we even friends?" I tease. Emma just laughs good-naturedly. "Are you nervous about cooking in a new space Monday? Do you know the setup?"

"Nah, I've gone over it all with Chef. He says it'll be set up similar to our kitchens at home, and I'm making the starter dish, so I don't have to worry about timing during the show. That's the hardest part."

CHAPTER SIX

⌯

Finding the set wasn't nearly as complicated as I thought it was going to be. Just as Emma's call sheet said, the beach parking lot next to the Santa Monica Pier was clearly marked. With the crew trucks and star trailers all lined up, it stands out like a sore thumb. One whole corner is completely taken over with a huge stage and a carpeted audience area, and tons of equipment trucks are parked in what must be the "backstage." Off to one side sits one of those gorgeous state-of-the-art mobile homes, which must serve as Hillary P.'s private dressing room.

Everyday Life with Hillary has been on TV for years. I can remember the girls in my college dorm obsessing over all the recipes and tips. I get it; she seems to really have it all. She's funny and charming with her celebrity guests, and when you watch her manage that clever arts and crafts stuff, you can tell she really knows what she's doing. I like to think I know a little about what goes on behind the scenes since Emma got the job as kitchen sous chef. She does all the grunt work of actually making the incredible food you see magically appear from the on-set oven.

The backstage seems completely chaotic as Emma and I approach the set of Hillary P.'s weeklong LA visit. Admittedly I don't have a lot of firsthand experience, but the few movie sets I've been on during beauty school weren't nearly as crazed. Everyone with a headset is running, all in different directions. I glance over at Emma, but she seems just as surprised as I am.

"I wonder what's going on..." The concern in her voice tells me it's not usually like this.

"The paramedics have already left." We both turn when we hear someone behind us shout into his walkie-talkie as he jets toward the fancy mobile home stationed near the set.

Emma grabs the harried-looking guy in the hockey jersey before he gets past us.

"Is it Hillary? Andy, what's happened?" Emma has to start speed walking to keep up with his pace to hear the answer.

"No, it's Bridget. Her appendix burst as she was setting up the trailer this morning." But that's all I hear before he's disappeared inside the trailer. Emma looks at me for a second before chasing after him. When she gets to the door, she glances back at me, standing still.

"Come on!" She waves me over.

"What are you doing, Emma? I shouldn't be going into Hillary P.'s private trailer!"

"She's not here yet, there's still time." She practically shoves me up the stairs and inside.

I look around the luxurious space, amazed at how roomy it feels. To the left is a makeup station complete with Hollywood lights glowing around the mirror. Several outfits are hung from a wardrobe rack set up neatly in the back.

"Did you call the guild?" The stressed-out guy, clearly the first AD, judging by the three walkie-talkies and multiple headsets clipped to his nylon vest, is being quizzed by a short woman with spiky, unrealistically white-blond hair. When she puts down the hair dryer cord she's untangling from several curling irons and faces us, I see she has about an inch of very dark, almost black roots. She must be Hillary P.'s hairdresser.

"Of course we called the makeup union, Monica. They can't magically snap their fingers and make a makeup artist appear here." Is it me, or do assistant directors always seem to be at the very end of their rope?

Monica slams a bag of eye shadows down on the counter next to the neat line of brushes. Obviously, the makeup artist had only started laying out her stuff before she got sick. There are a number of supplies set out in an organized row and then a whole bunch of things piling up in the center. Monica isn't even looking at the mess she's making, her eyes wide in terror at Andy.

"You know she's going to lose her mind when she gets here, right? When she finds out Bridget is not here, there is going to be hell to pay. And I'm not going to be the one to tell her. That's for damn sure."

I look over at Emma, who's listening raptly to the back-and-forth. I lean against her with my arm to get her to look at me. When she does, I mouth *Let's get out of here* as clearly as I can. This looks like a train wreck about to happen, and I for one don't want to be here to see it. Emma just shakes her head at me before concentrating on what the AD is saying.

"Monica, I know that Hillary doesn't like change. Of any kind. That's why I think you should do her makeup."

"Thank you for again proving that you don't know shit about what we do here, Andy. That is by far the dumbest idea I've ever heard." With nothing left to pull out of Bridget's kit, Monica finally starts trying to make sense of the makeup in a huge clump in the center of the makeup station.

"Um, Andy...I have an idea," Emma says into the fray.

"Not now, Emma. Can't you see this is serious?" When he turns back to the crazed hairdresser, I grab Emma's shirt.

"No!" I whisper in her face. "Whatever you're thinking, just...don't."

"Why not? You'll be great. Trust me!"

She shakes me off as Andy has abandoned all logic and is now pleading with Monica, "You've seen her get her makeup done a million times; can't you do it for just one day?"

"Number One has arrived. Three away from the trailer." The semi-encoded message alerts all of us to Hillary P.'s impending arrival. I have no business being in her private dressing room area, and based on the way everyone seems to be in terror of Hillary's reaction, common sense tells me that a stranger in her personal space will only make things worse. I feel bad for Monica; it's clear that no one wants to admit failure to Hillary P.

"Emma may as well do her makeup. You ever ice a cake, Emma? According to Andy here, it's the same damn thing." And then she's out of bravado. "I can't do her makeup. I'll try and I'll fail and then I will tell Hillary it was your idea and we'll both get fired. How about that?"

Andy glares at Monica, Monica glares back. And into the silent tension Emma pipes up, "My friend here is a makeup artist. She could totally do it." It's a full second before they both turn to look at Emma and then at me. If it weren't so serious, it would be comical how both of their faces change simultaneously from looking like they want to kill us for interrupting to looking at me like I just fell straight from heaven.

"Will you do it?"

"Is she any good?" *Now* Monica has time to be picky?

"She's good," I hear Emma say. I am utterly mute. She doesn't even glance at me as she whips my card out of her purse. "She'll do it."

"We've got maybe a minute before Hillary walks in here," Andy says, dead-eyeing me. "I'd like to be able to give her a definitive answer. Are you in?"

I nod my head slowly, not sure this isn't some crazy dream. Maybe I shouldn't have eaten dessert so late last night. I jerk when Emma elbows me hard in the ribs. "Oof. Yes. Yes, I'll do it." I look to my friend, who is now grinning hugely.

"Thank you so much, um...Alex?" Andy is reading off my card as he steps up and shakes my hand.

"Yes, hi. I'm Alex Cleary," I say, thinking he seems like a rational guy. I'll just explain to him my inexperience and let him decide. But before I can say anything else, the door opens again and in comes Hillary P. I've only ever seen her on TV, and she's much more petite in person than I'd imagined. For a second she seems exactly like the endearing talk show host and cooking guru she comes across as on TV.

But the instant she speaks she breaks the spell.

"Where the fuck is Bridget?" She tosses her huge Louis Vuitton shoulder bag on the leather sofa and sizes me up before dismissing me and turning to eye Emma. "Andy, why are they in my goddamn trailer?" I can't really get a read on her, though it's weird to have her talk about us as if we can't speak for ourselves. Obviously she's got a sailor's mouth, as my mom would say, but there isn't a lot of heat behind her words.

"Sorry about this, Hillary. But Bridget had to go to the hospital." Andy goes for a matter-of-fact tone. Before I can consider too much why he feels the need to apologize to Hillary about Bridget's illness, he goes on. "But we found the perfect solution. Alex just wrapped up the movie she was on. She was doing Jessica Biel's makeup." He looks at me to back him up, but with a split second to decide, I just can't do it. Hillary doesn't notice because she's busy settling herself in Monica's hair chair.

"No, um—" I start to explain. Emma and Monica both jump in.

"Don't be modest, Alex," Emma says confidently.

"It's Jessica Alba, Andy, not Biel. Idiot man." Monica backs up his story with a laugh. I turn to Emma, and she shares a grimace with me, but gives me a thumbs-up.

"I'm really sorry for being in your private space, Hillary. I just wanted to introduce you to Alex." Emma steps next to me. "She's been my best friend since high school. She does beautiful makeup."

"I'll know who to blame if she doesn't, right?" Hillary says it with a laugh, but I can see Emma trying to swallow past the lump in her throat.

"Well, you have such great skin, I would have to

work pretty hard to eff you up, Hillary." When in Rome, right? It's a risk, since all I know about Hillary is the very little Emma's let slip. It seems that Hillary is the type who'll eat you alive if she smells any hint of weakness. I'm only brave enough to hold her stare because it's just for today. I keep chanting that to myself. After a couple of seconds when everyone, including me, is holding their breath, Hillary lets us all off the hook.

"What's your name again?"

Monica gets to work wetting down Hillary's fabulously highlighted blond hair with water and begins massaging an elaborate concoction of products into her roots.

"I'm Alex." Taking Monica's lead, I dive into my temporary workstation. I meet Emma's eyes in the mirror. She mouths *Good luck!* I reply with a silent scream, but then smile to make sure she knows how grateful I am for this incredible opportunity. *Thank you.*

"Okay, bye," Emma says aloud. She winks at me and then is gone.

"Andy, can you clear my trailer?" Hillary demands in a very casual tone. I try not to flinch at Emma's quick exit.

"I'll have paperwork for you to fill out later, Alex. Thanks again for stepping in. You'll be done in plenty of time to get to that photo shoot you mentioned later. *Glamour* magazine, did you say?" And then, without waiting for an answer, Andy's gone. Leaving me alone with Monica and Hillary P.

I go for a laugh, hoping Hillary won't quiz me on any of the ridiculous lies he told about my résumé, but it sounds fake, so I just shut up.

"Did Wolfgang Puck cook for you himself?" Monica asks Hillary, drawing her into conversation. I send her a grateful glance, aware that she's rescued me, at least for now, with her distraction. Luckily, it's a story Hillary's been dying to tell, and she regales us with the tale of her delicious meal at Spago. Hillary's description of her sixteen-course experience with the head chef himself cooking sounds out of this world. Between cleaning up the scattered products and Googling images of Hillary P. to get an idea of how she likes her makeup done, it's easy to forget that Hillary never once asked anyone about Bridget's health.

CHAPTER SEVEN

"It's only noon on Wednesday and I need a cocktail. Is that bad?" I'm watching Hillary on the monitor backstage as Emma stands next to me putting finishing touches on a plate. This is my third day on the job, and somehow it already feels like a lifetime.

"No, it's a normal reaction around here. There's a cool bar near the studio where we all decompress after bad days," she says quickly. "You survived. That's what's important."

"You offered me up thinking I couldn't do it?"

"Of course not, I knew you could. But for a second there I was worried you would crack under the pressure."

I shoot her my best attempt at Hillary P.'s patented death stare. "I'm surprised she hasn't killed people with that stare."

"Well, you're here again today, aren't you? You chose to come back. Even after experiencing your first smackdown."

"I know. Don't remind me." Hillary laid into me the second we got back to her trailer last night. I never saw it coming, was so stunned, in fact, that I couldn't even remember all the details to do a proper play-by-play for Emma afterward.

"The director had to make me change my lipstick? What the fuck do you think your job is?" Luckily she didn't wait for me to answer that question; she just kept yelling. "You are supposed to check the monitors. You're the professional, you should know better than to put orange lipstick on someone with my skin tone. I mean, this is network television, for God's sake."

And then I sort of realized she'd stopped talking to just glare at me. Clearly expecting me to explain myself. "I'm so sorry, Hillary. It won't happen again."

"You're damn right it won't." She scoffed before taking off her high heels and tossing them aside. Next, her earrings skidded across the white countertop. Losing four inches did not detract from her intimidating aura at all. "Can you even explain what happened? I'm not interested in worthless apologies if you can't even figure out what went wrong."

"I thought my monitor was just a bit off. I checked it in the natural light before you went onstage. In real life it's just a bit coral is all, so I—"

"Well, real life doesn't matter, does it? When all of America could've seen me in orange fucking lipstick." And just when I was thinking about putting down my set kit and walking out—I didn't sign up to be her punching bag—she suddenly took in this huge breath and then came over to me. "Yelling isn't going to get us anywhere, is it? I just, well...I guess I have really big trust issues. And I thought I could count on you, that's all." Somehow she'd totally transformed from vengeful witch into hurt victim in front of my eyes.

"It won't happen again," I found myself repeating. "Now that I understand how the lighting affects things on set, I get it."

"Okay, okay." Hillary sighed again and then gave me a hug. Which was super awkward. "Everyone has a learning curve. And luckily Tom, the director, had your back today. But you can't always rely on that, right?" She turned her back to me, cleaning her face, looking at me through the mirror.

"Right, of course."

"And I just need to know you'll be there for me. Okay?" Hillary dropped the towel she'd been using and turned to me again, waiting for an answer. Her face, clean of makeup, reminded me how human she is. That of course there's stuff going on with her, just like anyone else. And the pressure is probably really intense. And for her to be honest with me about her trust issues, well, that really said something.

"Yes, Hillary. I won't let you down."

As the memory of how we ended things yesterday

echoes in my mind, it sounds oddly like a promise. One I mean to live up to. I'm discovering that being a makeup artist is kind of like being someone's shrink. Like maybe bartenders and manicurists, those jobs where people really open up to you. I probably saw a side of Hillary P. yesterday that most people never get to see. And it makes me feel oddly protective of her.

Back to the present, with Emma still going on about my temporary position on the show... "I only mean... Hillary doesn't like just anybody. It's pretty amazing that she let you stay to do the whole week. You should take that as a huge compliment."

"I do. Totally. Working this week on *Everyday Life with Hillary* got me into the union. I will always be grateful to her for that."

"That's a big thing?"

"Yeah, it's a pain in the ass, and everyone at makeup school talked about how that's the big hurdle. But thanks to you and Hillary, I'm in." I can't believe how it's all worked out. After this, it will be so much easier to get booked on jobs. So many opportunities require active status in the union, but no one will get you in. "I'm buying first round tonight."

"Sounds good to me," Emma says, but she's clearly distracted by her work. Jean Paul, the head chef in Hillary's kitchen, steps up to Emma and she is immediately 100 percent focused on her work.

As I head out to set during the commercial break, I evaluate my chance to get in close for a touch-up. I'm a fast learner; all it took for me to get the idea was Hillary biting my head off the first time I tried to touch her up while she was talking to someone. A simple "Not now" would have done the trick.

But Hillary P. keeps her cool in front of her live studio audience. I figured out quickly that she has no trouble putting on a cheerful, engaging smile for her fans while simultaneously compiling a mental list of mistakes to bitch you out about later in the trailer. Or having someone else handle the public humiliation for her. Apparently everyone on set has had their turn at this; I heard a bunch of stories afterward. But of course my turn happened at the end of the week of LA shows, in front of the more-handsome-in-person-than-is-fair Billy Fox.

FRIDAY MORNING I wake up ready to take on the world. My parents have made all their friends watch Hillary's show this week to support me. It's the first time they've really been able to pinpoint a career success of mine. It's already eighty degrees as I head to the location, and those dreary days of filing in the stuffy Pool Paradise offices seem like ancient history.

I go through the routine, snapping my hand out of Monica's way as she tugs on Hillary's hair while I'm trying to apply mascara. It's nice to feel a sense of confidence and pride about what I do.

I watch from my spot at the side of the stage, as Hillary does the first portion of her interview with Billy Fox. It's impossible not to be charmed by him. And not just because he's a movie star, either. Billy actually seems like a genuinely nice guy. I haven't seen a lot of his movies, but of course I know who he is. I've watched his fight sequence in the Tarantino movie in slow motion at least a hundred times for the special effects makeup on his wounds. It was so incredibly realistic. And that was before CGI. The makeup department on the HBO series he was on won an Emmy last year—there was one episode that had incredible age makeup on him in a flash-forward. He didn't bring an entourage with him, so I know his sexily mussed sandy blond hair is not the result of hours of blow-drying. And those sky blue eyes just naturally draw you in. No beauty school tricks there. His lashes really are that thick.

Hillary and Billy seem to be casually chatting during the commercial break, so it would have been easy to forget everything and just ogle the celebrity guest, as several of my coworkers were doing. I, on the other hand, pull myself together and casually walk up with my set bag to fix Hillary's lipstick. She lets me apply some fresh powder to her forehead, saying nothing, so I figure everything is good. I turn and offer to fix the shine on Billy's forehead (it gets really hot under the set lights), knowing he doesn't have someone watching him on set. Digging through my bag for a fresh powder puff gives me a second to recover from the charm of his smile. I've barely finished the touch-up when Andy is at my shoulder. I look at him questioningly.

"You need to get offstage now, Alex." I look around, perplexed. There is other crew still working; we obviously have another minute before countdown.

"Andy..." Hillary sounds hesitant. But somehow it means something else to Andy. Since I'm close enough to him, I see him flinch.

"Damn it, newbie. Get off my stage. We've got to go." Andy shoos me off the stage, yelling, "Someday people will understand what 'clear the set' means!"

Once he's hustled me backstage, I whisper, "Andy, I'm so sorry, I had no idea I was slowing down production. I didn't hear you call—" But he doesn't let me finish explaining.

"I'm the one who's sorry." He pats my shoulder. "I'll explain later." And he's gone off to cue the next food station to be brought to its mark on set. The show is back from commercial, live to the East Coast. As soon as everything is settled on the stage and things appear to be running smoothly, most of the crew breaks away from the backstage wings area, where you can watch the show, to rush back to their stations and get to work finishing the next thing. Emma and the rest of the kitchen staff are putting the final touches on some dishes that will magically appear from Hillary P.'s ovens, having been snuck in during the next commercial break, the flawless demonstration of "how to pull off a perfect baked ham, just in time for Easter."

Hillary summons me from the wings while the kitchen sneaks a perfectly finished Southern cherry pie into place during the last commercial break. It was an eleventh-hour addition because apparently it's a childhood favorite of her second guest. I rush forward but hesitate to touch her, since she's listening to the producer talk her through the celebrity's latest projects. "I need more lip gloss, Alex," she says before running through the questions she'll ask the starlet.

"Now?" I ask quietly. She looks at me like I'm nuts.

"Yes, of course now." So while she finishes up her powwow with the producers, I lightly powder her forehead and apply a fresh coat of lip gloss. When it's Billy Fox, lead guest, she doesn't want me to interrupt her, but when it's a rising pop singer, she insists on it. Got it. Andy's hurried explanation about Hillary's notorious mood swings is starting to make more sense. If her audience knew what she was really like, somehow I don't think they'd be as quick to buy her frying pans.

"But there's not a lot of union work right now." He wagged his wedding band at me. "I need the hours. Again, I'm really sorry about what happened earlier, Alex. But I think she kinda likes you, so if you can keep a low profile, it probably won't happen a lot." What the hell kind of advice was that?

"I saw the air show yesterday." It takes me a second to come back to the present and realize that Hillary's talking to me. I don't read her well enough yet to figure out if it's a good thing that she's paying attention to me right now.

"I thought you looked fierce. Were you happy?" I ask, picking up the thread of conversation. It's a risk, asking her straight out like that, but hell, it's my last day. I'm feeling reckless.

"I got a bunch of tweets about it, everyone loved it." It's not a straight-out compliment, but I'll take it. Then Hillary drops the bomb. "You're coming back with us. I told Andy today to work it out with you."

"Wait." I chase after her as she starts to walk off with one of the executives. "Are you asking me to come to New York and work on the show?"

"Well, I mean, you'd be an idiot to say no." She laughs as if she's joking, which I know she's not. When she realizes I'm not swooning over the offer, Hillary drops her smile and pushes away from the producer hovering at her shoulder. We're suddenly in a two-woman huddle. "I'm serious, Alex. You'll love New York. I know it's taken you a beat to get used to working for me, but like I said the other day, I need your fresh eye. Truthfully, I've been taking a lot of shit lately about my look being outdated, and you've made me look years younger. I'll make it worth your while."

"Yeah, okay." I'm dazed by the passion and sincerity in her eyes. And she did kind of open up to me the other night in her trailer; maybe a lot of her attitude is from loneliness, as my mom would've said. Obviously, I can't discuss this with my parents. I know they would panic at the first hint of my on-the-job struggles. I look to the producer, who clearly wants me to get lost so he can focus Hillary's attention on the up-and-coming pop star segment he's spent the week working on. I give Hillary a smile and retreat backstage to clear my head.

"She told you?" Andy is standing with his script in hand as I step offstage.

"Yeah."

"She wanted to tell you herself. You're lucky. She must really like you." Andy steps aside and quickly whispers to the audio guy adjusting the mic packs. I stare blankly, trying to figure out what to do. Do I want to move to New York? Is this a real offer? What is the offer, exactly?

"What about Bridget?" I ask Andy when he comes back over.

"She'll be taken care of, don't worry. But that's the business, right? If it's not you, it'll be someone else. Bridget's out." He must see the flinch I try to hide. "You gotta jump at the chances you get. You might not get another one." He leans away from me, talking into his headset. "Bring her up now. We're back from commercial in thirty seconds." He looks back at me.

"Don't question it. Just do it. It's a great opportunity. Come to New York. Figure out the rest later." Andy rushes off as our guest is brought up into the wings to go onstage.

He's right, of course. This is one of those opportunities my dad always talks about. When it knocks, you gotta answer the door, he's said at least a thousand times. I'll go to New York, I decide right then. For once, I'm taking charge of my fate.

CHAPTER EIGHT

"First round's on me." I raise my glass of syrah to toast with Emma's Appletini.

"Okay, but I'm buying next. We are definitely celebrating your new job! We'll use that car app—what'd you call it? To get home."

"Uber. Yup. It's an Uber night." We both drink deeply. And smile at each other.

"So, you'll stay with me, right? In the city, until you can find a place." Emma has it all worked out. She doesn't know that inside I'm cringing at how I'm even going to tell my family. She carries on as if it's all gonna be so easy. "I'll take you to the farmers market near my apartment. They have all sorts of stuff you can buy to make it feel like home for you."

"One minute I thought Hillary hated me and I wasn't sure if I was going to quit or get fired first. I never imagined she was going to offer me the job." I'm still reeling over it.

"She loves the big gestures." Emma smiles, but she's kinda distracted, too. I look behind me. "Don't *look*!"

"What?! What am I not looking at?" I turn back to Emma, but she's blushing furiously and staring at me. Determinedly not looking away. "OMG. What? I'm going to look for myself if you don't tell me right now."

"It's that guy. The guest from today's show!"

"You mean Billy Fox? He's here?!"

"Every girl here is staring at him," she says in a reverent voice.

"For the love of God, Emma. Please tell me you are not freaking out over a movie star."

"Are you kidding me? I binge-watched the entire *Wrong Doctor* series. Twice." She groans and laughs at the same time, snorting into her cocktail.

I sip my drink, not interested in being one of the ogling crowd. "I'm sure he's used to being stared at and fawned over."

Much later, Sean shows up, and the three of us hang out. By silent agreement, Emma and I do not bring up me moving to New York or Hillary P. offering me the job in front of Sean. It's a night for fun, and before long, Sean has pulled us both out onto the dance floor. We laugh and dance, like old times, until the band slows down for a couples' song, which of course is Sean's cue to claim exhaustion. He's never really been the slow-dancing type. He and I walk outside for some fresh air.

I lean in for a kiss when I see we're alone on the shadowed porch looking out over the crashing waves. He responds gently. But when he starts to pull away, I don't let him. I keep my hold around his neck and lean into him, increasing the pressure, hoping to spark some spontaneous passion from him.

"Hey, babe. What are you doing?" he whispers, hugging me tight, kissing my neck, but in a soothing way, not an on-fire-can't-wait-to-tear-your-clothes-off kind of way.

"I just thought we could, you know, enjoy the privacy," I whisper huskily.

"We're in public, Alex." Sean seems baffled. "Anyone could walk out here."

"Okay, let's go down to the water." I go for a lighthearted giggle, trying to seem carefree rather than letting him see how important this moment is to me.

"Wait, stop." Sean is a brick wall when he doesn't want to be moved. Once I'm not leaning against his body weight, he lets go of my hand. "What's this about?"

"What do you mean? Nothing. I was just having fun." Still trying to keep it light. *Fake it till you make it* and all that, right?

"Well, it's not fun to me. What is it with you lately? Like our sex life isn't enough for you? We have to do it on a gross public beach? You won't be happy till you get sand everywhere?"

Well, him saying it like that has definitely cooled my ardor to this idea. "Sorry, Sean. You're right. I was just trying to mix things up a bit."

"Why?"

"What do you mean, why? Obviously, you know... to keep things interesting. We're young—we should have wild, crazy sex stories to tell our grandkids someday." He makes a gag face. "Well, not that, but you know what I mean."

"Yeah, I do." He sighs, in a way that somehow seems very important. "Alex, I think you're not ready for a committed relationship yet."

"What?!" I'm caught completely off guard.

"Let me finish. I've actually been thinking about this for a while. I think we've both been pressured by your parents, and so settled down that maybe we're both missing out on the fun stuff."

"I don't feel pressured by my parents."

"I do." And the honesty of that hurts. A lot.

"Then why don't I let you off the hook right now. You do not have to date me because my parents want you to. They love you. They'd want you in the company no matter what." My fury is rising up to cover my embarrassment and hurt. "So don't worry about me, I'm fine. I definitely don't need to be held back by a boyfriend who doesn't want me."

"Alex, that's not it at all." He interrupts my tirade. "I

said this wrong, God. I do want you, Alex, I love you. I just think we should take a break for a while. You can try the single life, see what else is out there. And then we'll see if this is really the relationship we think it is. Maybe then we can settle down and get serious, you know?"

"Yeah, um." I am forcing myself not to cry. I can feel big ugly tears trying to push to the surface. Facing out to the water, I dig my nails into my palms and catch my breath. "Actually, I have something to tell you, too.

"Hillary P. offered me a job. To keep working for her." I start making a mental list of all I have to do this weekend to get ready to go, and with the TCA event on Sunday. (After humbly admitting to Hillary's assistant I didn't know what "TCA" meant, he explained in a superior tone that it was where all the media got together in one place—a day of interviews. It wasn't until later that I realized he doesn't know what the initials stand for, either.) That was added to my calendar last minute, that means I have just Saturday to pack before leaving first thing Monday morning.

"Really? That's amazing, honey!" He leans over as if to kiss me before quickly pulling back. Not soon enough for me to misunderstand what just happened. I wonder how cold the water is. I could totally pull a Shirley MacLaine right now and dive into the tide with all my clothes on. Maybe it's the wine I've had tonight, but I'm enthralled in visualizing Sean freaking out, yelling at me to get out of the water. Then I remember that I'm not in the ocean having a nervous breakdown, I'm standing on a romantically darkened balcony being broken up with. And my ex-boyfriend is still talking. What is he talking about? "I didn't know she was staying here. I thought you said she was going back to New York."

"She is," I say, remembering my news and now, of course, thrilled to have a reason to get the hell out of town. "Hillary wants me to go with her back to New York."

"Oh, that's too bad. I mean, to have to turn her down." I stay silent. Not the first time he's been wrong tonight. "Nice to be offered, though, right?"

"Actually, I said yes." I'm trying not to sound like a rejected girlfriend. This decision was completely independent of the bomb he just dropped, and he needs to know that. "This is a big opportunity for me, and I'm really excited about it."

"You decided to move to New York City without even talking to me first?"

"Well, obviously it's not your business now. Is it?" He gives a disbelieving snort, which I decide is an incredibly unattractive sound. "You know I've been wanting to get out of my parents' house for a while now, and this is really—"

"Oh, so that's it? You're not doing this to punish me for saying we need to take a break?"

I look at Sean, not extremely surprised that he could

be so egocentric. "Yes, shockingly, this is really just about me and my career."

"You mean your latest career? Last year you were going to be a bartender. And the year before that you tried applying for a nursing program. How long is this going to last, before you move on to the next?"

I have to catch my breath for a second at his brutal words. I've got to get out of here.

"I'm done with this conversation, Sean. You've made it clear we're not together anymore. So I really don't have to explain myself to you. Good night."

CHAPTER NINE

~ひ

After an insane Saturday filled with packing up my LA life and soothing my family's concerns, I'm actually happy to be working on Sunday. It seems like a pretty easy day ahead. I show up at Hillary's Beverly Hills hotel room at six a.m., following the instructions from Hillary's assistant's email exactly. I knock lightly on the door...after all, it is six a.m. I glance around the empty hallway, hoping not to wake her neighbors. No answer. I wait a couple of minutes, wondering if Monica is already inside. Maybe with the hair dryer going they can't hear me. I knock again, louder. Still no answer.

I check my watch. God, it's 6:10. I need to get in there. I text Cameron, Hillary's assistant, to let him know I'm outside the door. After a couple more minutes, I've decided to go back downstairs and call the room from the front desk when suddenly the door swings open. Hillary is wearing a baby blue silk tank top and matching short shorts, a sleep mask still on her forehead.

"Good morning, Hillary," I whisper, trying to be respectful of her obvious hangover.

She staggers back inside without replying. Judging by Hillary's matted hair, Monica's not here yet. I drag my wheelie carry-on suitcase full of neatly organized makeup behind me, following her into the suite. Her hair is sticking out in every direction and the place reeks of cigarettes. It's impossible not to gawk at the huge main living room.

"Where do you want me to set up?" I start to ask, but I hear the door slam and Hillary's disappeared into the private bedroom area. I'm setting up my stuff on the big dining room table when Monica lets herself into the hotel room.

"What the hell?" she asks by way of a greeting. "You should have started her fifteen minutes ago."

"Hillary just let me in," I reply defensively. "I was standing outside for ten minutes knocking."

"I didn't hear you," I hear from behind me. I spin around to see Hillary standing in the doorway, now wearing a hotel robe. "I'm so sorry I kept you waiting, Alex," she says in an exaggeratedly apologetic voice, "but there's no need to go spreading tales about it." Definitely feeling reprimanded, even though she said it in a casual tone, I rush to apologize.

"I'm sorry, Hillary. I didn't mean it like that." Feeling Monica's satisfied smile, I make a mental note that she definitely doesn't have my back. While Monica sets up her irons and fills her water bottle to wet Hillary's hair, I get to work on cleaning off the leftover makeup she clearly slept in.

ONCE THE SUV drops us off at the Langham Huntington, a five-star hotel in Pasadena, the morning is officially started with a briefing from Hillary P.'s publicist, a large woman named Rosalind Meeks. She chats with Hillary about everything from the weather to her latest TV binge until Hillary asks her for talking points for her interviews. I try listening for a few minutes, in case I need the information, but the glazed-over look in Monica's eye is a big hint that this conversation doesn't include us. So I turn my attention to soaking up the hotel around us. It's such a great piece of LA history. I almost share with Monica my story about our field trip to Pasadena in second grade to tour the famous Huntington Gardens, but she doesn't seem the type to appreciate it. It doesn't matter anyway, because we've arrived at the first interview area and within seconds of being in the tiny hotel room with no A/C, I immediately feel the walls closing in.

I take deep breaths as I touch up Hillary's pale lip gloss. While she chats up the Denver-based reporter, Monica and I do our last looks before the cameras start rolling.

Luckily Hillary has held up really well since we left her suite, so I don't think twice about excusing myself.

"You look great, Hillary. I'm just going to step outside for the interview," I let her know quietly as I put my brushes back in my set bag.

"What? Why?" she asks, clearly surprised; she's suddenly giving me her full attention. I feel like an insect under a microscope.

I glance around me. "It's pretty packed in here." Just seeing the limited space offered makes the room more suffocating to me. "I don't mind waiting outside."

"I mind," she declares, dead-eyeing some intern-looking person next to the audio guy. "There's plenty of room." And that's the end of the conversation. She gestures vaguely to the tiny corner where the camera guy has all his equipment stashed.

Okay, fine. I can do this. I plop down on the floor with my back to the corner, trying to give myself the most open view possible. My stupid battle with claustrophobia is not going to get the best of me. I have a job to do. While Hillary smiles for the cameras and chats with the reporter, I stare at my phone, playing Candy Crush to distract myself from the close quarters.

I survive the first few interviews like this, but each room seems to be getting exponentially hotter and tighter, and I know it's not just my imagination because Monica has huge pit stains on her T-shirt, and the crew guys complain about it every time an interview stops. We're not even at the lunch break yet, and it's getting impossible for me to breathe in the endless series of closets we get shut into. Finally, I decide to get ahead of this before I end up making a scene by puking or passing out during one of Hillary's interviews.

Before we head into the next torture chamber, I stop Hillary in the hallway. "Let me do your touch-up here. I'm going to use the restroom. Can I get you anything? A coffee?" I'm no dummy, figuring an offer to bring her back something might prevent Hillary's death stare.

"Oh, there's a bathroom in here I'm sure you can use," Hillary says from her upside down position as Monica sprays her hair into fullness. She flips back upright to smile at me. "Don't worry about the coffee, it's more important to me that you're with me. Cameron is bringing me a latte later." Rosalind gestures her into the next lockbox masquerading as a hotel room. With much less ceremony, Monica and I are shooed in after her.

By the end of her fifteen-minute window with the CNN entertainment reporter, the only thing keeping me from a full-on claustrophobic breakdown is my desperate need to pee. Maybe that's some sort of therapy I could recommend in the chat rooms I lurk in on sleepless nights.

"See," Hillary says, patting me on the back as she walks out, "was that so bad?" I look at her, not understanding.

"You don't like tight spaces, right?" She nods sympathetically at my confused expression. "It's okay, I saw it right away. You don't have to hide that kind of thing from me." And then she leans in close to me. I can't look away. "I can help you overcome it. This is your job now. Right? Use me to help you focus on something besides your fears. I really want to help you."

I think I nod in response, but I'm not sure. It's like being hypnotized. Hillary P. is going to cure me of my claustrophobia? It's hard not to be in awe of her arrogant godlike confidence. And then she's off. Cameron appears out of nowhere, latte in hand, and wearing fabulous Gucci sneakers, he sweeps Hillary into the next doorway down the narrow, windowless hallway.

By lunch, the tank top I wore under my sundress is drenched in sweat. I cannot breathe for the entire time we are in the horribly stifling hotel rooms. And the answer is a definitive no. Focusing on Hillary as if she is the messiah has not miraculously cured me of my condition. I finally ask one camera guy who's dripping in sweat why they can't turn the air on. After giving me a pitying look, he explains that the A/C makes too much noise for audio. It would ruin the interview.

No big loss, I think privately, as Hillary has basically regurgitated the same stories, answering the same six questions with the same fake smile, for the last five hours straight. And thanks to Monica and me, she continues to look picture perfect. Every time a tiny bead of sweat appears at her brow, I am there to mop it up. I've retouched her lip gloss thirty-seven times. I'm counting to keep myself from going insane in the impossibly tight quarters. Monica has given herself away as a cyborg who clearly doesn't need oxygen. I eye her suspiciously as she sits, calmly smacking her gum without a care in the world.

Once Hillary is safely eating her minuscule lunch, I hear Rosalind, the publicist, tell her she has twenty minutes of downtime, and I make a break for the great outdoors. I practically hyperventilate gasping in the fresh air. But after a few minutes of deep breathing, I'm finally able to appreciate the view from this patio. Below me is the breathtakingly expansive rose garden, with a huge stretch of grass beyond. I would love to go feel the grass under my bare feet for even thirty seconds; it would make me feel human again. But already I know better than to be more than a minute away from Hillary.

"Pretty spectacular, huh?" His bark of laughter at my reaction tells me that I didn't cover my surprised shriek as well as I thought I did. His charm immediately distracts me as he puts his hands up in the air as if approaching a wild animal. "Sorry. I didn't mean to startle you."

I don't think anything could have prepared me for Billy Fox appearing beside me in the cool shade of the huge bougainvillea. It definitely must be my overactive imagination detecting his subtle masculine aftershave on the breeze.

"Hi," I reply, because I can't think of anything better to say.

"You're Hillary P.'s makeup artist, aren't you?" How can he possibly know that? But before I can ask out loud, he fills in the blank for me. "I remember you from the show last week." Since I still can't think of one damn thing to contribute to the conversation, he continues, "I was a guest? On Friday's show?"

"Oh. Right." I finally rally to respond. "That looked like fun," I say moronically. "Making donuts."

"Yeah, it was," he replies, now looking at the view instead of me, which helps me think rationally again.

"What are you doing here?" Wow, Alex. Way to come up with a real conversation starter there.

"I'm doing some press interviews for the final season of *Wrong Doctor*."

"Oh, really? You're ending it? I've been meaning to watch. Everyone says you have to start from the beginning." I thought about lying and claiming to be a fan, but it seems like the kind of show I wouldn't be able to get away with vague details about. Emma isn't the only one who's obsessed.

"I'm really happy with how it turned out." He seems not at all offended by my honesty, which is nice. I side-eye his handsome profile as he leans against the railing, facing out toward the view again. "You'll have to let me know what you think."

"I will." And then, all of a sudden, I decide, why the hell shouldn't I flirt with him? I'm officially single. He's the hottest guy I will probably ever have the chance to talk to. I'm never going to see him again, so why not? "So you gonna tell me how it ends?" I say lightly, and shift my weight so my right arm brushes his as we both lean on the railing looking out at the roses.

"If I did that you wouldn't have any reason to watch," he teases. I'm definitely getting signals from this guy. And after what went down with Sean the other night, it feels good to have a guy look at me like this.

"I already have a pretty good reason to watch." Yes, that's officially the cheesiest thing I've ever said. The blush starts to rush in from my earlobes to heat my cheeks. And in response to either my horrible come-on or, more likely, my now embarrassed red face, I get to experience his adorably sexy laugh up close and personal.

"Okay, that's it. I have to know your name." He is giving me 100 percent of his attention now and my insides are melting from it. While I would love to keep the banter going, I really just feel grateful that I remember my own name.

"Alex. I'm Alex." And before I can do something stupid like reach my hand out for a handshake, my phone starts the Darth Vader theme music. There's only one person that could be. I silence it in my pocket without breaking eye contact. But as it turns out, my sense of self-preservation is so strong I'm about to walk out on the most sexually exciting moment of my life to respond to Hillary's summons. I stare into Billy's handsome face for one more second, trying to memorize everything about this exact instant. And then, knowing I will forever regret it if I don't take this once-in-a-lifetime opportunity... I reach up on my tiptoes and kiss him on the cheek. Relishing the instant of contact as much as possible without seeming like a stalker, I pull away just as quickly. "It was really nice to meet you," I say with complete sincerity. And then, wishing I had Cinderella's grace, or a glass slipper to leave behind, I rush back inside the green room of the Langham, back to real life.

WHEN I FIND Hillary, she's deeply involved in texting something while Monica recurls her blond layers.

"How much time do we have?" I ask Cameron, even though his ear is pressed to his oversized gold iPhone 6. It didn't take me more than one meeting with Hillary's fabulously dressed assistant to learn that if I waited for him to be off the phone to ask him a question, I'd wait forever.

"They want her for *Access Hollywood* in ten minutes,"

he answers automatically. Before I can turn away, he adds, "Oh, Alex, wait." Finally I have his attention. "I have some paperwork for you to sign."

I already signed my union papers and W-9 forms back at the show, so I'm not sure what's left, but I follow Cameron to his Louis Vuitton backpack, slung casually from a nearby dining chair.

"It's Hillary's standard NDA." He hands me the one sheet and a pen. Knowing I've got to touch Hillary up before she gets called back on camera or there will be hell to pay, I scan quickly over the paper, with no idea what NDA even stands for.

"Nondisclosure?" I read aloud.

"Yeah, it's standard with celebrities. I mean, you can't expect her to just share her secrets with you with her fingers crossed that you don't stab her in the back, right?" I can't help but see his point. Somehow my eyes land on a dollar amount halfway down the page: $5,000,000.00. "Five million dollars? Jesus. I don't have five thousand bucks, never mind five million."

"Well, then don't sell her story to TMZ, right? Easy enough." Cameron seems completely unfazed.

"Did you sign one?" I ask, thinking that'll be a good test.

"Yeah, of course. Everyone has to if you want to work in this industry." And he shoves the pen at me again, but his focus is clearly back on his call. Well, I guess that's good enough for me. This is my career now and I'm not really much of a gossip anyway. I definitely don't have Perez Hilton on speed dial or anything, so what am I worrying about? I hand Cameron the signed paper and he folds it into his backpack as if it's yesterday's newspaper. Obviously, these NDA things aren't that big a deal.

I walk over to Monica and Hillary, pulling out a clean makeup sponge and some under-eye concealer.

CHAPTER TEN

The rest of the afternoon is complete torture. I can hardly breathe moving from one tiny hotel room to the next. I try a few more times to avoid going into the rooms; staying out in the windowless hallways crowded with PR interns would be infinitely more tolerable than crouching next to the overturned bed, making space for all the lighting and camera equipment. Every producer clearly chose to shove the crew into one tiny corner to make it seem completely roomy on camera. It makes sense, but I do not have it in me to be logical right now.

"Hillary, you look great; once you're in there I can't really touch you up anyway, so I'm just going to stay here and catch my breath, okay?" She already called me on my claustrophobia, so I see no harm in admitting to the weakness now.

"No, Alex, it's not okay." She says it as if I'm a kid who's asked her for a second dessert. "I hate how hot those rooms are too, but I can't stop myself from sweating because you don't like closed spaces. I need to know I can count on you, even if it's not comfortable."

I want to tell her it's more than discomfort. It's a fucking phobia. Phobias by definition aren't rational. But maybe she's right—I've had more than one shrink tell me it's all in my head. Maybe this is just what I need to overcome this stupid fear.

"All right, of course. Sorry." I smile to let her know it isn't that important to me and we step inside the room. And into the suffocation chamber I return.

I TRY EVERY technique I'd ever heard of and a few more I Googled on my phone to distract myself from the situation. Nothing works. By the time Hillary lets me off the hook at six p.m., I'm completely mentally and physically exhausted. Even the thought of getting in my car to drive back to my parents' in the west Valley is more than I can handle.

Without really weighing the consequences of mixing alcohol with my frayed nerves, I step up to the hotel lobby bar and ask for a glass of pinot noir from the kind-looking elderly bartender cleaning glasses in the corner. The huge glass windows looking out over the lawn and setting sun help me breathe easier as I sit with my makeup bag at my feet, my purse tucked on my lap, and allow the wine to take effect. A few steady gulps and I know everything is going to be okay. I'll just have to learn to deal with stuff like this.

"Whoa…slow down there, tiger." I recognize his voice immediately. And my body temperature skyrockets as Billy Fox eases between bar stools to stand right next to me.

"Believe me. After the day I've had, I need it."

He signals the bartender over and orders a Bass Pale Ale on tap and a second glass of wine for me, which is when I realize mine is empty. Then he gently herds me off my stool to an empty rounded booth next to the gorgeous bay windows. Admittedly, I don't put up much resistance. "Okay, what'd Hillary do now?" he asks when we're alone.

Immediately I think about the confidentiality agreement I signed today. Even though he's definitely more famous and successful than Hillary P., this is probably exactly why she has people sign them. And anyway, my phobia isn't her fault.

"I just have trouble in enclosed spaces," I admit, trying to simplify my ordeal. "Today…all those hot, airless hotel rooms kinda got to me."

Billy's delicious smile immediately turns to concern. "Is this booth too tight? Do you want to go outside?" He looks around as if to arrange just that.

"No, I'm fine, really. The windows help. I can totally breathe down here. I don't know why today triggered it." Not true, of course; I know exactly what—or rather who—triggered it. "I haven't had an attack in a long time."

"Are you sure you're okay?" he asks again. His hand squeezes mine on the table.

"Yeah. Thanks. I really am much better now." I want to look into his eyes, but I learned at lunch that I turn into a dummy doing that. I'm better off swirling my wine.

"I'm glad," he says. "What made you claustrophobic? Was there an incident?" he asks after a few minutes of silence.

"Yeah. It's kind of an embarrassing story, though." I don't know why I would even consider telling him this story.

"Those are the best kind." He leans back in the booth, enjoying his beer, enjoying teasing me. "Come on, you can't just leave me hanging..."

"I got stuck when I was a kid. There was a bunch of publicity and stuff. Firemen had to get me out. I don't really remember all of it, but apparently it was pretty traumatizing." It's getting easier to talk to him, and while I'd like to blame the wine, it's Billy. His easygoing manner has captivated me and put me completely at ease at the same time.

"Sounds like it." He gestures the bartender over, and they chat like old buddies. It's impossible not to be charmed by how respectful Billy is to the server. Before I know it, I've committed to a couple of tapas from the bar menu and another round of drinks. I remind myself that with my new job, I can afford to Uber home if I want to. Once we're alone again, he pins me with his bright blue gaze. "I think there's more to that story, Alex." His knowing grin and the way he says my name with that Texas lilt is more of a turn-on than I could've imagined.

"Isn't that enough? I mean...I was on the local news and everything. A little claustrophobia is nothing, really." I nod my thanks to the bartender as he sets out silverware and a plate of tuna tartare.

Billy uses the placement of food as an excuse to slide closer to me in the curved booth, and now I can feel his warm thigh against mine as he prepares a cracker with tuna and avocado relish and puts it on my plate. "Tell me," he says, leaning in. His proximity would make any heterosexual female crazy. It's the only explanation for why I confess a story to Billy Fox I haven't told anyone about since sixth grade.

"I got trapped," I begin. Another big swallow of pinot and the rest just babbles out. "In a claw machine." I see that he doesn't understand. "You know, those toy machines at the arcade? You put money in and try to get the claw to grab you a toy? Yeah. Apparently my parents weren't really paying attention at Chuck E. Cheese's and I climbed into one." I keep talking over his stifled laughter. "It happens more often than you'd think. Back then it did anyway. They've probably figured out a way to stop it from happening now." He's now hiding his smile behind his beer mug. As if I don't know. As if it doesn't make him even cuter. "It's not funny, the firemen had to break the whole thing to get me out."

"I'm sorry, you're right. It's not funny," he says sincerely. And then he ruins it by adding, "I bet you have a thing for firemen now, too." I do, but really, what woman doesn't? I mean, I don't really think my childhood fiasco has anything to do with liking a guy in uniform.

"I don't chase firemen, if that's what you're asking," I say indignantly.

"Are you dating anyone?" Billy Fox, getting to the heart of the matter.

"No," I answer truthfully. "No, I'm not."

THIS WHOLE NIGHT is completely surreal. Billy made me forget he's a movie star before the appetizers arrived.

The lights go down when the live band takes over the hotel's main bar lobby. Billy finally gestures that he can't hear me anymore and actually looks disappointed. I must be imagining that part. I awkwardly fiddle with my cocktail napkin, wondering what happens now. I don't have any practice in flirting, but I know for sure I don't want this night to end. And somehow I have this crazy inner confidence that Billy feels the same way. But just in case, I offer him an out. "You probably have to get back to your hotel." I look for our server.

"Don't you dare be lookin' to pay for dinner. I'm buying," he says. "And I'm not ready for this night to end. I don't have to drive—I'm staying here."

"Really?" I ask, surprised.

"Yeah, I don't need to be put up at some fancy Beverly Hills hotel. I like Pasadena. Reminds me of home." He looks me in the eye. "You shouldn't be driving, either." And he means it seriously; it's not an invitation.

"I rode here with Hillary, so I was going to Uber back anyway. But I can stay for a while." And then there is no doubt. He takes my hand and leans in so his lips are right up against my ear.

"Wanna dance?"

I feel his body heat even as he pulls away to see my response. I give an enthusiastic nod. And in the next breath, he's slid out of the booth and then pulls me to my feet. It's so dark now, it's hard to make out his features, but the LED lights occasionally flash over us as Billy pulls me out onto the packed dance floor. We find an isolated little corner, and maybe it's the wine or the company or the night, or maybe some mystic combination of all of the above, but I'm just enjoying the chemistry with a gorgeous guy who is clearly as into me as I am into him. We dance and sweat and sing along to all the same classic songs.

When the band starts the opening beats of Queen's

"Somebody to Love," I turn to Billy and feel my insides melt when I see my excitement mirrored on his face. He grabs me around the waist and we face the stage. His body tucks in behind mine and he sways us to the beat. In the dark, lost in the crowd, it feels so good and easy to just lean back into him and go with the flow. And from there everything changes. Even as the beat picks up for the next couple of songs, we are glued to each other. He's turned me back to face him, my arms fall naturally around his neck, and his hand is on my lower back, holding me against him. I've officially lost all sense of time.

He takes my hand with a casual Texan chivalry and escorts me back to our table. Billy tosses a few large bills onto our check. My whole body is buzzing, feeling his warmth next to me. And then we're off. By the time we step into the elevator, I am so charged up and he hasn't even kissed me. We're alone so I'm able to breathe normally, riding up in silence. Billy is leaning against the opposite wall, but his eyes are searing into mine, keeping my attention on him and not the walls closing in on me.

"I think if I kiss you right now, I'm not going to be able to stop."

I add mind reading to his list of good qualities.

I am more turned on now than I have ever been in my entire life. I feel more desired now than I ever felt with Sean. I banish the thought of my ex from my brain—I'm not going to let him ruin this experience for me.

In an instant we're arriving at the double doors leading to his suite. He swipes his key card and the door clicks open. Billy gallantly steps back to let me through.

"Wow. It's beautiful." Billy has let us into a completely decked-out suite. The Mediterranean-style hotel has designed the rooms with luxury in mind. We're on a landing looking over a gorgeous eight-seat dining room table in rustic walnut; the guest bathroom to our left, decked out in gold fixtures and marble countertops, makes a pretty fancy first impression. Behind it is an archway that must lead to the private kitchen. On the right is a seating arrangement in front of an oversized fireplace.

I don't notice I'm frozen in place until I feel him move in behind me. His hands land on either side of mine on the railing and I can feel his breath on the back of my neck.

"I'm glad you like it," he says against my ear.

"Do you have dinner parties here? What's with the dining table in a hotel room?" I really don't know how to be sexy. There's no point even trying. Obviously Billy doesn't mind because I can feel him smile as if I just said the perfect, most attractive line in the book. He kisses my ear, then nuzzles my neck, and instinctively I stretch my neck to allow him more room to play.

"I mean...I can see how people need a place to host, I guess...if they're staying here a long time. I didn't mean that it's not super cool. I mean, it is...super cool...

I just—" I'm still babbling as Billy grabs my hips and stops my words by spinning me around so my back is against the rail and my front is pressed right up against his. And then he's kissing me. No hesitation, no introductory, tentative, warm-up kisses. It's just one never-ending incredible, deep, soul-searing kiss.

Everything that happens after that is a blur, because he never stops his mind-drugging kiss. I know I throw my arms around his neck, running my fingers through his hair, letting him know the only way I can that I don't want to stop kissing him. Ever. He responds to my silent yes by lifting me up, pulling my thighs around his hips. And I hold on tight as he carries me down the hall. Since he didn't break the kiss, I have no idea where we are. All my attention is on him. But when I land on his bed, I can't wait for what happens next. And it is everything I never knew I wanted until now.

I WAKE UP with a start and realize two things immediately. Billy Fox's arm is draped around my naked body, holding me close to him, and the bright digits on the alarm clock in front of me read 4:37 a.m. I have a flight to catch. Oh God. I immediately tense up, realizing that if, God forbid, I hadn't woken up, I'd have missed my flight to New York, not to mention being stuck with some horrible morning-after scenario with Billy Fox.

It doesn't take me but a second to conclude that last night was the best night of my life. Hands down. And the last thing I want to do is ruin it with some awkward conversation where Billy has to get rid of me. It's easy to slide out from under his sleep-slackened arm, but not as easy finding my clothes strewn around his darkened room. A hundred memories come flooding back as I gather up everything I was wearing yesterday by feel. I tiptoe into his bathroom and switch on the light only after I've shut the door. I pull up the Uber app and discover with massive amounts of relief that even at four in the morning, there are several cars just five minutes away. I order one and quickly dress. Feeling my way through his room toward where I remember the entrance being, I dig into my purse and rip a sheet of paper out of my pocket-sized notebook. I write quickly, glancing at my watch. The last thing I want is to have the driver leave if he doesn't see me right away.

Thank you for the perfect night. XX Alex

My pen hovers over the page while I consider leaving my number. But in the end I decide it's just too tacky. Plus, how long would I spend staring at my phone, hoping he'd actually call? Better to make a clean exit. I put the note in the center of the dining room table, where I'm sure he can't miss it. And like the conscientious girl I am, I double-check his door is locked on my way out.

CHAPTER ELEVEN

I've been in Manhattan for forty-eight hours, and other than eating late-night take out and sleeping at Emma's, I've only really seen the inside of Hillary's West Side studio. I am itching to get out and explore anything beyond Times Square. I want to see the city, I do, but I haven't quite wrapped my head around Emma's tour guiding idea.

"We're walking up Fifth Avenue," I repeat. The words are English, but the meaning hasn't sunk in. "All the way?"

"Yes! I think it would be such a great way to introduce you to the city." Emma checks her watch. "I'm going to have to get back to the kitchen; my copycat Cinnabons need to come out of the oven."

"Okay, but let's talk about this, Em. That sounds like a really far walk..."

"Oh, stop. You Angelenos, you love to exercise but you won't even walk next door. It'll be great. You'll love it." And she's disappeared through the studio doors, heading into her backstage kitchen area.

Hillary is with Monica now, getting her hair done. Monday they aired a repeat to give Hillary a chance to travel home. But first thing Tuesday morning I was thrown into the deep end of making a TV show, and I knew no one was going to take the time to teach me to swim. At first I hung out with Monica and Hillary in Hillary's thankfully spacious dressing room, trying to soak up everything I could learn from them regarding the show as they made small talk. I also want to make sure Hillary knows I am happy to be here, and happy to be at her beck and call. But now that Monica knows she's stuck with me permanently rather than when I was just helping out in LA, she's made it clear that she doesn't want me in her way while she's working on Hillary. So today, Wednesday, I decide to stroll the hallways, grab a cup of coffee, and chat with Emma for a few minutes during the hair-drying portion of Monica's work. That machine gets so damn loud, but Hillary doesn't seem to care, she just raises her voice over the roar of the dryer. Not only does she talk nonstop about her life, her friends, and her enemies, but she definitely likes us to validate her choices, her snappy comebacks, and her decision to bitch out her useless agent.

It's a tricky thing, 'cause I know she likes that I don't fawn all over her, but she also clearly values unquestioning loyalty above all else. There's no doubt that a client like this needs to know I'm on her side no matter what. I've definitely done some soul-searching over the past two days in this new city. I've lain awake at night wondering if this was the right decision. If I can handle working for Hillary. And the answer is a resounding yes. I know I can put up with anything because this is my dream. For too many years I've sat back and watched my siblings work tirelessly to make their dreams come true. I have it in me to do that too, I just had to find *my* dream. And now I have, and I'm not going to let anyone, including a selfish, egotistical TV personality, keep me from it.

When I get back to the makeup room, they're still on the same bitch session as when I left fifteen minutes ago.

"I don't give a shit what the network executives say. They don't know what goes on here. They don't know what I need. They shouldn't have a say in who I have working for me, period."

"You're totally right, Hill." Of course, Monica has probably done nothing but repeat that sentence all morning. It took me less than a day on set with Monica to realize she is Hillary's lapdog. I'm watching my back around her, 'cause I know she'd take even the smallest thing back to her boss. She's put the hair dryer away, and is running a big-barreled curling iron through sections of Hillary P.'s blond locks, creating her signature messy chic look.

"Sorry to interrupt, but Hillary, do you want me to get started? We have about twenty minutes before your producers' meeting." Hillary came in about half an hour late today, but she still expects everything to run on time.

"I knew I loved you, Alex." She blows me an air kiss, which means I'd better start mixing up the foundation I'm using on her skin. I start by gently applying a really expensive moisturizer on her face. She's closed her eyes, so she doesn't see that Monica has brought the curling iron incredibly close to the back of my hand. We are, out of necessity, in each other's work space; I get that. Trying to minimize my obstruction, I've squeezed in between Monica and the counter, but I freeze up seeing how close I just got to getting burned. When it's safe to look up at Monica to see what the hell that was about, she's already setting her irons down and moving on to tease Hillary's roots. It didn't seem like an accident, but maybe I'm overreacting. And I can't really address it, since Hillary's already back on her current topic.

"Rosalind is my hire. She's done the PR on my books, and I like her. She's been handling the show just fine."

"And really, what do they know, right? I mean, it is your show, Hillary. You would know how to run it. Not the network." Monica offers a new variation on her practiced yes-man answers.

"What is the network saying? Are they saying there's a specific problem?" I can't help it. I should probably butt the hell out, but I mean, I'm stuck here until I've got her false eyelash strips glued in place, and so far Hillary's been into my opinions.

"They say she doesn't do enough to promote the show. Which is stupid. Obviously, I want her doing the book stuff. That's her focus. But I can't exactly say that to the network."

"Look up," I instruct, cleaning leftover mascara from underneath her eyes. "Isn't it important for her to do both?" Monica shoots me a dirty look, which I ignore.

"No. I just want Rosalind to sell my books." Out of nowhere, Hillary is a brick wall.

I don't respond, since obviously there's nothing else to say. I get out this beautiful shimmery face powder that feels so soft and refreshing when I brush it on. "Close your eyes," I murmur gently.

When I first started doing makeup, I got the idea that it was in some ways very similar to being a facialist or even a massage therapist. When women put on their own makeup, usually it's rushed, slapped on roughly. I knew from the beginning that I wanted to create a peaceful, relaxed feeling. There's always a fabulous scented candle in my kit, although I didn't have time to light it today. Maybe I'm an eternal optimist, but I like to think these few seconds of peace will help Hillary be slightly less bitchy as she goes through her day. It's a nice thought anyway.

I have a soothing routine I've developed with all my

clients. First I apply a face serum, then an all-over jasmine healing cream. Then I put on an SPF 50 primer, which helps the foundation stay on, and then a little dab of a stress-relief eye cream—it has caffeine in it, which helps with puffiness and hydrates the sensitive skin around the eye. Obviously, I could go on and on about this stuff for hours. I don't always go step-by-step with my clients; they need to just relax, or memorize lines, or do whatever they do to prepare for their day. Usually I can sense from their vibe that my routine has helped center and calm them, and that makes me feel like I've done my job right.

When Hillary breaks the silence several minutes later, it's quickly clear that the ball-busting Hillary P. has resisted my Jedi mind trick. "The show promotes itself," Hillary proclaims. I see Monica in the mirror smirk as she's putting her hair sprays away. I've clearly brought up an unpopular opinion. It would have been better all around to just not get involved.

"What makes you think she's not doing both?" Hillary says after another minute of silence. Now that she's completely reversed her earlier opinion on Rosalind, I'm torn as to how to reply. I softly wipe powder across her forehead and over each eye and gently brush it down her cheeks. Taking my time applying some Aquaphor to her chapped lips before carefully selecting eye shadows, I am still trying to navigate a response.

This time Monica catches my eye and shakes her head

quickly. It's good advice. The hairs on the back of my neck are standing up in reaction to Hillary P.'s casual question. Her tone is too unassuming; I'd be a fool to ignore the warning signs. If I got fired my first week because of my big mouth, my family would never let me live it down.

"What do I know, Hillary? I do makeup." I laugh, lightly brushing on her eye shadows, going for the simple style she loved in California.

Monica shakes out Hillary's curls, jerking her head, and I have to pull my hand back quickly to avoid stabbing Hillary in the eye with my brush. I glance at Monica, but she's completely focused on Hillary. "This feel right today, honey? I like it down with the neckline of your dress." She's brushing Hillary's hair forward and running her fingers through it again to demonstrate the fullness of the style.

"Yeah, I love this." Hillary turns her head first right and then left, examining her hair from all angles. Monica holds up a hand mirror so she can see the back too, which immediately changes Hillary's expression from a pleased grin to a grimace. "It's too fucking flat here, Monica. Look at that, there's a huge hole in my hair." Hillary twists her body so she can see the back of her head better in the mirror. She presses her palm down on one section of hair toward the back. If it wasn't flat before, it is now. "You'd have to be blind not to see it." But Monica nods in automatic agreement.

"I see what you mean. I'll get that. But you like the style, you're okay with this for today?"

"Once you fix that chunk, yeah." And both the hair and Monica are dismissed from Hillary's mind as she retreats to checking her emails.

With her eyes lowered and her head relatively still, Monica pulls out a section of hair to recurl it. I meet Monica's eyes and mouth *Thank you*. I know she brought up the hair to change the subject. I could've really gotten in trouble. And while I'm still sure that Monica isn't my friend yet, I think I've made some progress with her at least.

I ORDER UP a glass of wine for Emma and one for myself at the bar around the corner from the studio. She said it would only take her a couple of minutes to get her pineapple ham in the oven for tomorrow's show. TJ's looks like the perfect place to slow down and relax. I feel like I haven't stopped moving since I got to the city. But the old stained wood décor, cozy leather booths, and slouchy tables create the perfect dive-bar comfort.

"Are you gonna drink both of those?" asks the cute guy two stools over from me at the bar. He was nursing a whiskey-looking drink when I walked in. I definitely noticed his short ponytail and tattoos. But after the Sexual Experience of a Lifetime with Billy Fox, I'm thinking I should swear off men for a while. It wouldn't be fair to any guys who came after Billy anyway.

"No. One's for my friend." And then, needing to clarify, "She'll be here any minute."

"Well, so you're not drinking alone." He raises his glass and leans over to toast with me. His effortless smile puts me at ease that he's not expecting anything from me. And knowing that Emma is coming any second, I don't worry about passing the time in conversation with him. "I'm Nick."

"I'm Alex." I reflexively check my phone.

"Oh, sorry." He looks at my phone. "I don't mean to intrude." And he goes back to his paper.

"That was rude. Sorry," I say right away. "I'm from LA. It's a nervous habit," I add self-deprecatingly. It's easy to distract him with the obnoxious stereotypes New Yorkers have about people from Los Angeles. And I feel bad for having offended him.

"It's no biggie." He smiles again and I'm suddenly taken by how attractive he could be. I wonder what he would look like if he cut his hair shorter. "So..." He gestures to the wine I'm nursing. "Long day?"

"Yeah." I sigh. It's nice to talk to someone who doesn't know what I do. "I have kind of a crazy boss."

"Tell me about it," he says rhetorically. He toasts me again and polishes off his drink with one hand while gesturing for another. "And it's only Wednesday."

"Exactly." I commiserate with another long sip of delicious escape.

"So, what brand of crazy do you work for?" he asks, concentrating on squeezing his lemon into the cocktail and giving it a good stir.

"Oh, the usual kind, I guess." I don't want to get into Hillary, really, but it feels good to get this off my chest. "I think today, she was setting me up."

"Your boss was setting you up?" he asks, and I finally have his attention.

"Yeah, I shouldn't have offered my opinion about..." How do I put this without giving away what I do or who I work for? "One of her other employees." He snorts at me. "I know, it's none of my business. But I just felt, you know, I shouldn't stand by while she's getting taken advantage of."

"Where do you work?" he asks, getting into my story. Damn it, I didn't expect him to be this interested.

"I really shouldn't say." When he seems confused, I explain, "Confidentiality and all that."

"Oh, of course. Well, you haven't said anything bad yet." He continues to look at me, as if expecting the rest of the story, even though he knows I'm not allowed.

"Well, I guess it was nothing, really. It was more just a feeling that if something hadn't distracted her, she was going to bite my head off for trying to help."

"Well, if you worked for me, I'd be thrilled that you

were trying to protect me. But, to each his—or her—own, right?"

"Yeah, right." And it feels nice that he thinks I did the right thing bringing it up, even if Hillary didn't. "What about you? What do you do?"

"I work here. In Midtown. I'm in finance at Hearst."

"Is that stressful?" It's hard not to look at my phone wondering where Emma is, but now that he's called me on it, I can't.

"Not really. Actually, I love my job, but right now I have an opportunity to move up the ranks."

"Well, you should take it." I smile, moving on to the glass of wine I'd ordered for Emma. He laughs when I take a sip.

"To making the most of every opportunity." I raise the glass in a toast I've never meant more.

Emma appears in the door, shrugging off her coat and settles in between me and the cutie. I'm about to introduce them, but he's moved away while I was distracted saying hi to Emma and ordering her another glass of wine. And as she downloads me on the latest kitchen crisis, I notice he's paid his tab and disappeared.

CHAPTER TWELVE

April

There are so many things I've come to love about New York in my first weeks here. Riding the subway isn't one of them. I absolutely loathe the entire experience. I feel short of breath the second I begin walking down the stairs, so I try to avoid it as much as possible.

For most of the touristy things Emma and I have done, we've splurged on taxis. We got last-minute tickets to see a few Broadway shows after work. Emma took me on a quick walk through Central Park, but we were rushed to get back since I only get a thirty-minute lunch break. Between settling in to a new city and working for Hillary, I just haven't had time to do everything on my sightseeing list yet.

The biggest adjustment so far is that New Yorkers walk everywhere. I quickly realized my flip-flops were not going to cut it on these busy city streets, and had to upgrade to Chuck Taylors. Dragging my wheelie full of makeup equipment is no easy feat, either. But once I got a sense of the geography—streets run east/west, avenues north/south—I pretty much figured it out.

Tonight, though, here I am with no option but the subway because I am running late for "girls' night." I have bonded more quickly than usual with this group of women Emma introduced me to for one very good reason—baseball. I haven't quite worked up the courage to admit it to my LA family, but one of my new favorite things to do in New York is go to a Yankees game. And I'm willing to withstand a subway ride for it. My childhood shrink would be so proud that I've finally found something worth battling my claustrophobia for.

I don't feel disloyal heading up to the baseball mecca. I need baseball in my life. With the new season beginning, I've decided to root for the Yankees in the American League and the Dodgers in the National League. No judgments here, people, I can be whatever kind of fan I want to be. And until they square off in the World Series, I don't see a problem. Slipping my MetroCard into the turnstile while avoiding touching anything is a new art form. I'm also a bit of a germaphobe, but really, that's not a phobia, that's having common sense.

I listen to music with earbuds so that I can pretend not to hear people talking to me on public transportation. I've been out to the stadium three times now, and each time I've arrived relatively unmolested and climbed the stairs to my StubHub seats in the nosebleed section with a beer and popcorn. Both are items I would never normally partake of, but I used to get nachos at the Dodgers games with my dad and brothers until there was a terrible losing streak, after which they made me swear never to order nachos again. I switched to popcorn and we won, so I'm just being respectful of my new local team's mojo. I'm not really superstitious. It just seems an unnecessary risk. And I like popcorn, so everyone wins.

Harriet, Emma, and Missy have four season tickets for Friday night games. I was lucky that they had a fourth friend drop out last minute, so I scraped together the money to buy into the tickets. They all seem like cool chicks. I of course met them through Emma, so they're pre-vetted. Emma has a pretty good instinct about people; I've grown to trust it over the years.

"Emma! Did you know Hillary P. is throwing out the first pitch tonight?" I hear Missy asking as I scootch down the row to join them. Missy's married to a trader on Wall Street. Sometimes her husband gets hooked up with tickets in the Dugout Club. Which we are appropriately jealous of, but she enjoys the nosebleed section with us just as much.

"Alex! You made it!" I accept high fives all around for successfully navigating the New York subway system solo.

"Your boss is so cool," Harriet chimes in. Emma and I exchange a commiserating glance but say nothing. Harriet is a spin instructor at SoulCycle. "You're going to be at my class tomorrow, right? Got to burn off those nasty popcorn and beer calories!"

"I had no idea she would be here. I can't believe everyone wasn't talking about it today," Emma says, getting us back on track. I'm embarrassed that I didn't know. Hillary had me touch up her makeup after the show today, showed me this revealing blue top and black motorcycle jeans she was going to wear, and told me to make sure she looked super sexy. Why wouldn't she tell me this is where she was going? I take a picture of her close-up on the Jumbotron and zoom in as much as possible on my phone, proud of how hot the cat-eye makeup looks.

Settling into my seat, I hope that my confused feelings about working for Hillary don't taint the Yankees tonight. Leave it to her to actually throw the pitch all the way into the catcher's glove. Of course she did. Hillary P. doesn't do anything unless she can do it well.

"Popcorn?" I offer to the group. I hate that I missed the national anthem. I like the pomp and circumstance at the start of every baseball game. I'm not as hard-core as Missy; she showed up an hour early to watch practice. Emma usually waits for me, but when Hillary asked me to stay late (without getting overtime pay, by the way) I encouraged everyone to go ahead. With my eyes on the field, I pull out a pen and open the program to keep score.

My dad taught my brothers and me to keep score practically from birth. I know...it's weird. I used to see several other, usually older, men keeping score like me. But in the last few years, my dad has stopped going to games as often. When he doesn't give the seats away for business reasons, I take advantage. In our section, everyone knows I'm the one keeping track.

I watch the first couple of innings with complete concentration. There's something so peaceful about the Yankees decimating their American League opponent. While the other team warms up a new pitcher, I take a moment to appreciate the *Lost* numbers hanging there on the retired Yankee jerseys.

"You want anything? Alex?" Emma pulls me out of my zone during a switch in pitchers.

"No, I'm good." I haven't touched my beer. And the popcorn is half gone from being passed around.

"Okay. Text me if you need anything. We'll be right back." As all three girls inch past me, I turn my knees to the side to let them by, and accidentally lock eyes with a guy who's been sitting near us. He is clearly from the Bronx; his accent as he's been shouting out batting advice is a dead giveaway. I go back to reading my program without acknowledging him. Unfortunately, he seems unwilling to take the hint.

"How's it going? I'm Gary." He leans over the seats made empty by my friends. And I get a fresh whiff of his cologne mixed with sweat.

"Great game." I smile and gesture to the field. The relief pitcher on the other team has finished warming up and the Yankees are at the top of their lineup. Apparently drawing his attention back to the game is a futile endeavor.

"It's gonna be a great season. Yankees are looking good." He seems determined to extend our chat. "You're a big fan?"

"I am." I gesture to the notes I've been taking. "Looks like Tanaka is shaping up to pitch another no-hitter." And then I return to marking up my score sheet.

"From your lips…" Gary chuckles deeply. I can sense him looking for a new topic, and I know I can't do anything until my friends come back. "So, it's just ladies' night tonight?"

I'm not a big fan of lying. It's not that I'm morally against it or anything, it's just that when I try to lie I always seem to make things worse. Case in point: With an overly friendly Yankees fan, I could: (a) make up a story about a longtime boyfriend who is a Mets fan; (b) say I'm a lesbian (And then, what? I just never bring a guy to Yankee Stadium? No way.); or (c) stick to the truth, no matter how it hurts.

"I just haven't met the right guy yet," I tell him. At first he smirks, thinking it's an opening. But then he surprisingly, insightfully realizes I'm including him in that statement. I'm holding my breath until, amazingly, he backs off.

"Well, when you do bring him…he better stay the whole game. That's how you'll know he's the one." He laughs again. And sits back in his chair, turning to his friends. But somehow his pronouncement stays with me. He makes a good point. I can't stand people who leave before the end of the game. Even when it's clear we don't have a snowball's chance in hell of winning, I stay. I've never left a game in LA early. I wonder for a second if Billy Fox is the type to leave games early. I'd like to believe he hangs in to the end, rain or shine. But that's probably just wishful thinking.

"YOU LOOKED GREAT on the Jumbotron at the game on Friday!" I say enthusiastically to Hillary first thing Monday morning.

"What the fuck are you talking about? I got crucified all over the Web for it," she responds from behind huge bug-eyed sunglasses. I don't have a Twitter account yet, but it occurs to me I should check out the Internet before opening my big mouth and pissing her off.

"How is that possible? Everyone around me at the game thought you looked hot." Once Hillary gets on track it's impossible to change her mind about something, but I have to try. "And most of them didn't even know I work for you." There were plenty of wolf whistles from my section of the stadium, so it's not a lie.

"Look at this. Just look." She jams her iPad in my face, and I almost can't focus on the picture she has pulled up. I take the tablet from her to get a better look. "I look like the goddamn Joker, Alex. What were you fucking thinking?"

The picture was clearly taken outside the stadium; it must've been at the end of the night, because almost all the curls had fallen from her hair. The humidity came on heavy after ten o'clock. I see exactly what Hillary is referring to, but at first I can't understand how it happened. I look at her helplessly before zooming in on the picture again.

"Yeah, look at that fucking disaster close-up. Dear God, you know America expects me to be perfect, right? I'm not going to let you fuck up my image, Alex. You're lucky I don't fire you right now."

There's definitely a burst of adrenaline from her threat. At this point I am completely dependent on her paycheck to survive in Manhattan. And . . . "I don't know how this happened." There are three white streaks on her face, one on each cheek below the eye and the other bright as day across her forehead. It almost looks like she'd put on war paint. "You looked fantastic on the big screen during the game. You couldn't see these streaks at all. Is it your powder?" I think aloud. "It must be."

"Of course it's my damn powder. How could you give me something that would do that?"

"Well," I offer hesitantly, "did you blend it in?" She inhales deeply. "I mean, you know, you must have applied it after you threw the pitch, right? Did you use the brush I gave you? You have to kinda smooth it all in."

"You think I don't know how to apply my own damn makeup? Of course I blended." She's worked herself up into a rage and now blindly grabs something off my makeup station to hurl across the room. It doesn't land near me, and given her perfect aim at the game, it's safe to assume she didn't mean to hit me. When I feel the words "What the f—?" about to explode from my mouth, I just run out of the room before she hears them, leaving my broken mess of liquid foundation all over the floor, spreading to her faux fur area rug.

Once in the hallway, I take a bunch of deep breaths, trying to figure out what to do. It's like the tenth time in just weeks that I've thought about quitting. Hillary must be bipolar. She's a maniac. But I manage to keep reminding myself of the big picture here. I don't want to go back to LA; it would be totally humiliating to explain, especially because I wouldn't really even be able to tell my parents why Hillary P. is a nightmare to work for. That damn confidentiality agreement—no wonder Hillary demands everyone sign one. I'm surprised she's not the lead story in *Star* every week.

After I pull myself together, I realize I'm just going to have to suck it up. I know it's not my fault that she didn't fix her makeup right as she was leaving the game. And she knows it, too. She's just embarrassed and has to take it out on someone. It's not that big a deal. I go into the crew kitchen area and grab some paper towels. But I decide that the next time I'm alone with her, I'm going to tell her I draw the line at throwing things. I don't really care if she yells. But I'm not going to just lie down and become Hillary P.'s doormat.

"HE'S SUCH A JERK. I'm so sorry." Emma puts down the slider to hug me again.

"I know. Sean is a total jerk. I mostly just wish I hadn't wasted so much time on him." We're drowning my latest embarrassment in bar fried foods. TJ's around the corner from the studio has become our nightly hangout. "He was with my parents too, you know? They were all on the phone together telling me if I can't handle my first job in Manhattan I should just come home."

"Total douche move," she concurs wholeheartedly.

"But I can't even really blame them. It just sucks 'cause I'm not going to explain to them what's really going on with the Dragon Lady. I'm sure I just seemed like this vague, whiny brat who couldn't hack it in the big city."

"Do you want to go home? Really?"

"No. Absolutely not." I am completely firm on this, which of course is totally at odds with how upset I am. "It just makes me feel like I've wasted all this time with someone who obviously doesn't know me at all. I mean, Sean didn't even really try to figure it out. They all just assumed I would fail here." I take another onion ring and add, with my mouth full, "It's very depressing."

She nods to the TV behind the bar, which has some sort of cage match playing on mute.

"Want to watch something else? We could see if the Dodgers are playing,"

"I want to take my mind off him. And Her. But I doubt even baseball will do the trick tonight."

"Oh my God, Alex. I never heard how things went with Billy Fox! You have to share every juicy detail!" Emma demands. And of course, I do have to. I couldn't have kept it a secret from Emma for a thousand NDAs.

"He's amazing."

"I knew it! OMG, Alex, I'm dying..."

"We talked forever. We danced." I pause, remembering how it felt to be in his arms. "He's a really good dancer. And he likes eighties music."

"Oh, thank God. He can live," Emma says sardonically. "So...then..." She rushes me along. "Get to the good stuff!"

So, I go into as much detail as I can, and I know

I've done a good job distracting us from my family crisis because Emma's fanning herself when I finish.

"Good lord. So has he called you yet?"

"I didn't leave my number," I say as casually as possible.

"You said you wrote a note!"

"I did. I wrote something like, 'Thanks for an amazing night.'"

"How could you not leave him your number?"

"He's not going to call me, come on. Let's be realistic here. He's a movie star, right? I'm just...me."

"But you didn't even give him the chance to. I mean, Alex...why wouldn't he be totally into you? Just because stupid Jerk Face"—our new nickname for Sean—"is a complete idiot doesn't mean every guy is."

"Well, it's over now. I don't have his number either, so I won't be tempted." And just to get us off the topic, "What time do you have to be at work tomorrow?"

After we work out the logistics of our morning commute, Emma reminds me she has to pop back to the studio to prep her bird for tomorrow's show. I get a glass of water to sober up a bit while I wait for her to get back. In New York, taxis are the perfect designated drivers, but I'm too old to be getting hammered on a school night.

"Wow, you're getting soft on me, Alex." I smile back at Nick as he shrugs out of his jacket and sits down next to me, ordering his drink. "Water? So early?" I'm starting to feel like a local, recognizing the same people in TJ's all the time. I love that I have friends in New York already.

"Nah, I've had my fill. I'm just waiting for my friend, and then we're heading out."

"Well, you look good, Alex. I mean, as good as anyone can look on a Monday."

"Yeah, it was definitely a Monday."

"Your boss again?"

"Yeah. I got bitched out for something that totally wasn't my fault. And I just had to suck it up. Which… sucks." I crunch on some leftover ice.

"That totally sucks. I'm not good at that—I'd probably mouth off and get myself in trouble."

"Believe me, I thought about it. I fantasize about it. But I know I'd lose my job in a heartbeat."

"Well, at least you're free until tomorrow. She lets you sleep, right?"

"Except when she calls me in the middle of the night," I mutter.

"Okay, now I'm dying to know what kind of shitty job you got yourself mixed up in. What are you, a spy? You get midnight phone calls?"

"Nothing as cool as that…" What can I say without giving too much away? "It's never about something important. She just vents to me on the phone. Sometimes about things I do that she doesn't like… um, later, when she thinks about it." Yes, Hillary DVRs her own show and then watches it in the middle of the night to critique everything. I'm probably not even her first phone call.

Nick is looking intrigued, but I know I shouldn't say more. It just feels so good to be able to have him see what I'm going through. And since he has no idea what I do, it feels safe to vent a little. "I just think...this woman I work for...might be bipolar or something. Sometimes she gets so irrationally bat-shit crazy, and other times, I don't know...I feel like I'm seeing through the BS to the real her, you know?"

Nick is in listening mode. I'm not sure why I feel I can talk to him more than I can Emma. Probably because Emma is in it, too; she's chosen to work for Hillary P. for years, so it feels weird questioning whether I can make it through another week. "Maybe I'm just fooling myself. Who knows?" I see Emma through the window. "Okay. God, it's almost ten o'clock. Maybe I'll see you tomorrow. Good night, Nick." And I rush to meet Emma at the cab.

CHAPTER THIRTEEN

"Alex, hi." I turn around, unwilling to believe what my ears are telling me. There is Billy Fox. Casually strolling toward me down the studio hallway, as if we run into each other every day. "Just the person I was looking for."

"Hello, Billy," I say, since I can't think of anything better. Emma was grilling me about him last night and now here he is. We summoned him.

"It's nice to see you." He takes the expression literally, as an opportunity to look me up and down. Every time I imagined running into Billy Fox again, I envisioned myself in some fabulously trendy dress ripped from the cover of *InStyle* magazine. Which clearly did not happen. My kooky tie-dyed Chuck Taylors, a rebellion against the close-toed shoe policy, actually look normal compared to my MC Hammer–style sweats and the three tank tops I layered instead of wearing a bra. In my defense, I was looking for a passive way of marking my independence from Hillary without actually getting myself fired. I never for one minute thought I was going to be seeing Billy Fox today. Or ever.

"I was hoping to see you that morning in my suite, but you disappeared on me." His Southern drawl is thicker than usual.

"I, um, I had a flight to catch. I wasn't trying to sneak away." Which of course is total BS. Luckily, Billy is kind enough not to call me on it. "What are you doing here?" I've got to take control of this conversation.

"I'm doing the *Late Night* show," he says, as if he's just an average Joe out getting the newspaper, not a huge movie star who gets top billing on any show he wants. There are several TV shows running out of these studios. In Manhattan everything is packed together. "Are you done for the day?" he asks me, as if he has nothing but time to chat. I'm sure there are like nine people from the crew of *Late Night* looking all over for him.

"Me? Oh, um...no. I have to pack up my kit to take to Hillary's. I'm doing her makeup for some event tonight." I'd been griping to Emma that it would've been nice to have some advance notice, since I had to cancel my first dinner down in SoHo for this. I was also complaining because I had to come back to pack up my stuff. But suddenly I'm very grateful for Hillary's last-minute demands.

"Well, I'll let you get back to it." But he doesn't move, just stares into my eyes some more. And even though I'm standing here without proper undergarments on, I just do not want this moment to end. He really is staring into my eyes right now. I don't speak, because I am truly tongue-tied. He finally breaks the silence. "I'd like to buy you dinner sometime."

"Really?" I ask honestly, before I can stop myself.

"Yes. Really." He takes my phone from my hand. It's still open to my iMessage conversation convincing Emma that this walk up Fifth Avenue she is determined to make happen is basically akin to hiking Mt. Everest.

He chuckles at what I wrote—"Sorry, I couldn't help but read it"—as he backs out and finds the Contacts app. "I felt the same way when I first came here. We like our trucks in Texas."

"I thought you were gonna say horses," I say, doing a terrible impression of a Southern twang. Which makes us both laugh.

I watch him add his cell phone number. "Call me when you have a free night. I'm going to be in New York for business in a couple of weeks. I would love to see you." He leans in and kisses my cheek and then walks past me toward the elevator bank. I stay still, faced away from him, until it seems safe; he must have rounded the corner by now. And it's a solid minute before I can pull myself off the wall I leaned against because my knees wouldn't support me.

I stare down at my phone with his number in it. I don't

know what to do. Panicked, I hit edit and scroll down to the delete icon. If I get rid of it now, then I won't give in to temptation and call him. But I can't bring myself to do that. I stare at it a second longer, before an incoming text lets me exit out of the app, leaving his number intact.

THERE ARE A bunch of things about living in New York that are still so damn frustrating. I miss my car so much as I haul my makeup kit up the steps at the Upper West Side subway station closest to Hillary's fancy Central Park West address. I've heard about her home a half dozen times already, and I know it's going to be worth it just to get a peek inside.

I've gotten better about walking with purpose through the crowded sidewalks, which took me a while to figure out. But now people move out of my way, as opposed to the almost apologetic sidestepping I was doing at first. It's not my natural mind-set, so I chant motivational catch-phrases to distract myself as I see a particularly large group gathered, waiting at the light for the row of cabs coming out of the park.

Hillary's building has a fancy doorman in uniform, like it's a hundred years ago. He's super nice and rushes forward to help me get my bulky bag through the doors into the lobby.

"Go on up, Miss Alex. She's expecting you."

"Thanks, Victor." I smile, reading his name tag, and take the fancy elevator he gestured toward all the way up to the penthouse floor. It's one of those tiny, old-fashioned elevators. I try to pay attention to the ornate moldings and fixtures, but I'm still sweating a bit as I step out into Hillary's apartment. The tight feeling from the tiny elevator box is immediately relieved by the huge open space around me. I mean, it's probably the same square footage as my parents' house in Northridge, but this...is different. Every window has a stunning view, mostly of Central Park, with the buildings of the Upper East Side towering behind the greenery.

She obviously has a professional interior designer. The whole place has hardwood flooring, with these oriental rugs creating "conversation areas." I sneak a few pictures on my phone while waiting for Hillary. Obviously I'm not going to send them to anyone, but I figure next time I'm with my mom I can show them to her; she would especially appreciate the attention to detail evident in every corner.

"Alex. There you are. My car's coming in twenty. I cannot be late." Twenty minutes? Why the hell didn't she have me come sooner? But of course I don't voice this question aloud.

"Where do you want me to set up?" I ask calmly. I've learned Hillary does not handle other people's stress well. She leads me into her expanse of a bathroom, where there's a huge vanity mirror with makeup lighting and a wide marble counter for me to lay out all my stuff. But of course there is no time for that today. Hillary sits in her custom cushioned makeup chair as I dig out her foundations and quickly start mixing up her base color.

"What are you wearing tonight?" I ask, getting right to business. I brush on the combination of foundation and bronzer to even out her skin tone and create that dewy glow she loves.

"A black Chanel dress," she answers, already typing on her phone. For once, I'm happy about her digital distraction because it will at least keep her still, which makes my job easier. It's usually a nuisance when she's typing or playing word games because to apply makeup I need her cooperation.

"Look up," I say, the foundation brush poised under her eyes. She ignores me for several seconds, finishing a text. Then she looks up. I barely keep my sigh from escaping. I probably have less than seventeen minutes at this point to get her done. Keep focused, Alex. "Do you want to go glam? Or keep it simple? What's the dress like?"

"It's the black strapless that drove everyone mad in Paris this year," she brags dreamily. My reaction is more confused than impressed. "Fashion Week?" she prompts me, which of course does nothing to help me figure out what the dress looks like. I feel the clock ticking away like I'm failing my eleventh-grade chemistry final all over again. "It was on the cover of *Vogue,* for God's sake. Plebeian." She huffs, starting to get out of the chair.

"Stay," I bark before my sense of self-preservation can stop me. Her eyes widen at my tone. Which makes my stomach tense, but I know better than to back off. "I've got less than fifteen to get you done, Hillary. You don't want to look like I rushed."

"All right, all right." She settles into her chair, and while a part of me is freaking out that I schooled Hillary P. and got away with it, I remind myself it's not over yet. She'd better have a perfect face or I'll get shredded.

Without asking any more questions, I decide to go for an Old Hollywood glam look. Very clean eyelid, lots of dark lashes with a bright red lipstick. I realize as I'm trying to draw the thin black eyeliner across the edge of her lashes that perhaps I should've done this style on a day when my hand wasn't trembling. I take a break in the middle to steady my right hand with my left.

"Look at me." I've finished lining both eyes and need to make sure they're even. She looks into my face as I examine my work, with a Q-tip ready for any incremental changes. Hillary briefly fills me in on the event she's attending tonight.

Still concentrating on cleaning up the tiny winged edge of her left eye, I murmur a reply without really listening.

"They're putting my new cookbook in the goody

bag." Brushing another coat of super-black mascara into her upper eyelashes is impossible while she's talking, I hold the brush away from her eye, and that's when I notice a bit of tension there. "I'm making a speech, actually, and accepting an award."

"That's great," I say, uncomfortable with the idea that she needs or wants a pep talk from me. "Congrats." But by the time I think of anything else to add, she's on her phone again, so I must've misread her. Maybe her Botox is fading. Finally satisfied with the look of the positioning of the dark strip of lashes I added, I grab my lash brush. "Look straight."

Before I can even tell her I'm finished, she stands up and leans into the mirror, examining her eyes and the red lipstick. A loud, old-fashioned ring echoes through the apartment. She grabs the closest extension from the bathroom. "Okay." She hangs up. "My car is here."

"Let me help you dress," I offer, since there's no one else here. I hadn't really noticed the absence until just now. I wonder why Cameron isn't clucking around her. Does she have a boyfriend? Hillary P. normally has a small crowd of people constantly buzzing around her at the show. Maybe she likes having peace and quiet for once. I try to look nonchalant as she casually strips her clothes off and shimmies into the gorgeous black dress she's pulled off the hanger.

She presents her back to me and I start to pull the zipper up from her waist, but it's too snug. Holy crap. I instantly panic. This is a nightmare I never even imagined. I am completely unprepared for what to do if this damn dress doesn't fit. I try not to let her see I'm freaking out. Pulling the two sides in tight, I think it'll close, but I need an extra set of hands. "Can you just push the edges together here?" Without comment, Hillary does, and I manage to force the zipper all the way up without breaking a sweat. Maybe it was meant to be tight, since she didn't freak out about it. She pauses to preen in front of the mirror.

"Fits you like a glove," I say to fill the silence. And it does look spectacular as I step back to take in the whole look. The Chanel silhouette is stunning on her, especially after she slides into her sparkling silver Louboutin four-inch peep-toe stilettos. I take a minute to appreciate how perfectly my makeup complements the dress. "You look fabulous."

"I love it," she tosses out while grabbing a matching clutch from the puffy stool in the center of the walk-in closet. Was that a compliment for me or Coco Chanel? As she walks to the front door, she says over her shoulder, "You can let yourself out." I follow her toward the door, somewhat stunned that she's leaving me alone in her apartment.

"Have fun," I say awkwardly.

"Always," she replies, letting me see her paste on her bon vivant smile. She steps into the waiting elevator, and when she turns there is no hint of the irony from moments before. I wonder at the glimpse behind the mask she's shared with me. It feels like progress.

CHAPTER FOURTEEN

May

Not even Monica's crappy attitude can ruin my good mood this morning. It's been impossible to wipe the smile off my face since I woke up. Things have been going great. Hillary and I have found a rhythm that seems to work. And while I can't dodge every arrow she slings at me, I like to think I'm developing a tough skin. Something my parents never thought possible. And finally, last night, having Emma's apartment to myself for once, I worked up the courage to call Billy. What started off as a tentative conversation from my end quickly turned into an all-out late-night heart-to-heart. It was sexy. It was sincere. I would never have believed how easy it was to open up to him. And when I could hardly keep my eyes open, curled up on my side with the phone tucked between my pillow and my ear, he promised to come pick me up after work today. We're going on a date.

Billy: What time you think you'll be done?
Me: We have pickups after the show so, 6 pm? Is that
too early?
Billy: not soon enough.

I kept rereading his texts during the show today.

"Hey, Alex. The boss wants to see you." I've just finished cleaning my brushes from this morning when Andy pops his head into the makeup room. "She's in her office." Monica looks at me gleefully.

"Okay, Andy." And he's gone before I can ask any questions. I can't help but respond to the smirk Monica doesn't even try to contain. "What? What are you so happy about?"

"It's never good news when you're called into her office." She makes sure all her irons are off before prancing away. "Let me know how it goes," she calls out as she disappears around the corner.

Since I can't imagine what I could possibly have done wrong—well, other than the usual criticisms about how I missed a spot when I touched her up between commercial breaks—I'm not particularly alarmed at this point. Hillary reviews every minute of every episode for flaws and has made it clear I'm expected to do the same. Even though I watch it happen from the monitors onstage, during my first midnight phone call from Hillary she insisted that I be current on how viewers see the show at home. I swear to God, she's even quizzed me on edits to make sure I really watched it. Two nights ago we discussed her conviction that I must have used a different lipstick to touch her up after act three because "Clearly," she insisted at two in the morning, when I was too vulnerable to defend myself, "it's an entirely different shade of nude."

Since it's way too soon for Hillary to have reviewed today's show—we just wrapped fifteen minutes ago—maybe it's good news. Maybe she loves the paparazzi photos from last night's event. I certainly did. Since this time I had more time to prep her, and Monica had done this kick-ass vintage hairstyle, I was refreshing my Twitter feed every few minutes looking for pictures of Hillary at the Women in TV celebration. The pictures I found online looked fantastic. It was pretty cool, actually, to see my work under the glitzy lights of a red carpet.

Arriving at her dressing room door, I knock softly.

"Come in." Hillary isn't alone. There's an older man in a conservative suit that completely clashes with the chic floral print sofa he's sitting on. He doesn't even look up at me when I walk in; he's focused on some papers strewn on her delicate, antique-looking coffee table.

"Andy said you wanted to see me?" I ask, since Hillary isn't really saying anything.

"Yes, I do." She sits down in her plush armchair next to the suit.

"Do you remember signing this?" he asks, all business. I'm starting to get the picture that this isn't going
to be a cheerful conversation; the guy hasn't even introduced himself. I take the paper he's holding out to me.
It's my confidentiality agreement.

"Yes. Of course."

"Then you know you owe me five million dollars,
you little—"

"Hillary." He holds up his hand, which, remarkably,
actually stops her short. "I'm Douglas Fircham. Hillary
Pinche's attorney." He gestures for me to sit in the cozy
overstuffed armchair positioned at the end of the coffee
table. Not knowing what else to do, I sit. "It has come
to our attention that you have violated the terms of this
agreement. So your employment here is immediately
terminated. And we will pursue legal action if you do
not produce the liquidated damages you agreed to pay if
you violated the agreement."

It's like he's not even speaking English anymore.
This Fircham guy doesn't even have an unkind face. He's
definitely older, midsixties. But he has that trustworthy
look about him. I hear the seriousness of his tone, but
nothing is processing. "Wait, you think I talked to someone. About Hillary? I didn't!" Now that I've figured out
what they're accusing me of, I quickly work to defend
myself. "I swear, Hillary, I didn't. I would never!"

"We know it was you, Alex. Don't bother denying

it," she spits at me. Clearly the guy has been her lawyer for a long time; he is completely unfazed by her outburst and simply puts a calming hand on her arm to keep her... in place, I guess. She looks like she's about to attack me.

"Why would you think that? Hillary, come on!" I see on her face that she doesn't believe me, and I desperately try to come up with a way to defend myself.

"I am going to make sure you never work in this industry again," Hillary says, completely unaffected by my pleading innocence.

Determined to get someone to listen, I focus on the lawyer. His freshly shaven face shows wrinkles and laugh lines, so he must have a heart. "Why? Why do you think it's me? I haven't even been online today, I don't even know what you think I might have said."

"Your lies are not helping you here." He calmly gestures to Hillary's irate face. "We know it was you because you're quoted as a source. Hillary was given the final copy of Nicholas Slants's 'unauthorized' biographic article on Hillary for *Identity* magazine. The magazine was hoping for a response from Hillary to add to the piece." I'm hanging on his every word, waiting for anything he says to make sense. "She was quite shocked to see that you had provided specific stories. Not just your grossly exaggerated description of Hillary's character, but you recounted incidents that only you would've known about. Of course it was you."

"But I didn't!" I say again. My eyes fly across the pages of the printout he's handed me, and there it is. All spelled out in black and white. My name, my words. I slowly read every line, thinking somehow it can't be true. I didn't even tell my parents my horror stories about Hillary. "Late-night phone calls" and "bipolar" leap off the page at me. Nick. My friend from TJ's. The guilt swamping me must be written all over my face. "I never told him your name. Hillary—I swear to you—I never even told him I worked in TV. How did he know?"

"If what you say is true, then he set you up." Mr. Fircham collects the pages from my numb hands. "Which makes your crime no less egregious. You agreed to the terms and now you've admitted to violating them."

"But not intentionally!"

"My firm will be contacting you to make arrangements to initiate proceedings to collect the five million dollars."

It's impossible to think straight. My heart is slamming against my chest. My whole life is flashing before my eyes. "Hillary, you know I don't have five million dollars! Not even close. I can't pay that."

"You should have thought of that before you stabbed me in the back," Hillary shoots back with venom. "You will be destroyed for this. I will sue you for everything you've got. I will garnish every paycheck you ever earn at whatever minimum-wage job you find for the rest of your miserable life. You're going to have to hand it all over to me. Now get out." Hillary turns her back on me, and her lawyer takes my elbow, steering me toward the door.

"Wait! Wait!" I slip out of his grasp and run around the chair to lock eyes with Hillary. But I see there is no use. I'm nothing to her. Fircham is by my side in a second. This time with a firmer hold on my arm, he starts me toward the door again. "Give me a chance to stop it. I can stop him." I don't know what I'm promising, really, but I grab hold of the idea with everything I've got. "Hillary, you don't want my money. And even destroying me isn't going to change anything once this story gets out."

"If you think I'm going to let you get away with ruining my reputation—validating his story, you've lost your mind."

"But what if I can stop the story from coming out at all? Then your reputation isn't ruined, right?" I must be saying something worthwhile, because the lawyer has stopped trying to physically remove me from her dressing room. "Just give me a chance to stop the story from being published. If I can do that?"

"Why should I?" she spits.

"You think you can succeed where my entire legal team hasn't?" Fircham looks skeptically at Hillary.

"You're never going to work for me again, no matter what."

I let that pass, as if I would want to after this. But I'm fighting for my whole life here. "But you won't sue me for the money? Right? If I find a way to stop that article from being published, you won't do anything to stop me from working other places?" The room is so quiet I can practically hear Hillary's wheels turning as she considers my offer.

"I'll give you two days."

"What?" That's no time at all. "Two days isn't enough—"

"We have to start damage control. Forty-eight hours is all we can afford to waste on this folly," Fircham interjects. "Ten o'clock Friday morning, if you're not here with proof that this problem has been eradicated, I will file the paperwork."

Clearly the friendly, fatherly lawyer thing is a façade. His words are laser sharp, as clearly he takes my offer as somehow undermining him.

"Okay, fine. But if I stop this story, that's it? You won't come after me?"

"I'll draw up an agreement stating such, Ms. Cleary. But you only have until Friday morning. You'd better get moving."

I look at Hillary, wanting to hear it from her.

"I don't break my word." That stings as much as she wanted it to.

CHAPTER FIFTEEN

ى

I've finally ditched the security guards that watched me pack up my makeup kit and escorted me to the lobby. They were actually quite polite, but that didn't stop it from being humiliating. With Monica watching over her station as if I was going to steal something from her, I'm glad the guards were there or I might have slapped that smug smirk off her face.

I roll my suitcase toward the doors, hardly aware of the people moving through the building around me. The ringing in my ears is so loud my eyes start to blur with tears I absolutely refuse to shed. When I stop to wait my turn to get through the revolving doors, a firm hand grabs my arm.

"What the hell?" I lurch back, expecting Hillary or her goons on the attack.

"Alex. I've been calling your name. How could you not hear me?" I am now blocking the flow of foot traffic. It's hard to focus on Sean's face, even though he's a foot from me.

"Sean. What are you doing here?" I'm completely gobsmacked.

"I came here to see you, obviously," he says with a chuckle, pulling me away from the exit. Here we are in the bright, sterile lobby of the building where I just got fired. I don't even know if I'm allowed to still be here. And now my ex-boyfriend is hugging me as if we were forced apart by external influences rather than him breaking up with me.

"I just didn't expect to see you here. I had no idea you were coming to New York." I put a question in my voice, hoping to get him talking so I can get my mind to reboot.

"I'm here for a couple of days, a big convention in New Jersey your dad wanted me to attend." That sly grin that I used to think was so adorable now has me wondering if this is what a quarter-life crisis feels like. "He wanted me to check on you while I was out here. Make sure everything was 'on the up-and-up.'" Sean lowers his voice and does air quotes for my dad.

And suddenly it all seems so easy. I could just tell Sean everything. Well, not everything...just the relevant details. He could tell my dad for me. They would bring me home. Hire a lawyer, I don't know. They would make it all go away.

"Hey, honey...is everything okay? You look kind of pale." Sean puts his hand on my forehead to feel my temperature, the way a mother would. And somehow that seals the deal. Even if I end up working at a pharmacy selling ninety-nine-cent lipstick, I'm not going home to be treated like a little girl again.

"I'm fine, Sean. It's just been a crazy morning." He nods as if waiting to hear more. "You know, early hours. It's brutal, really. But I love it!" I say with all the enthusiasm I can muster.

"I'm so glad, Alex. Can I come see where you work?" he asks, looking back to where the security guards watch the elevator banks. I follow his gaze only to realize that several of the guards are still eyeing me suspiciously. Oh God. I've got to get out of here.

"Actually, I'm on my way to do a personal makeup. I'm running a bit late," I say apologetically. "If only I'd known you were coming!" I throw in passive-aggressively.

"Of course. Of course." Sean grabs me by both shoulders and hugs me again. "I'll be around for a couple of days. When your schedule clears up, text me." He looks me straight in the eye. "We really need to talk. Okay?"

"Yeah, okay. I'll text you." I smile as I head to the doors, forcing myself not to check to see if the guards are still watching me. Luckily it's an off time, so several cabs are winging their way up Broadway, and I flag one down before collapsing into the backseat.

My mind is a mess as I scramble to exit the taxi and

force myself past the swarm of tourists spilling out onto the busy street. Navigating pedestrian traffic has become second nature already, but my mind is occupied with desperately trying to figure out my next move. Finally I track down Emma—with no choice but to accept her offer to join her one-woman walking tour up Fifth Avenue.

We're already well into the walk before I work up the courage to tell Emma what happened. At first her outrage on my behalf gets us odd stares from the foreign tourists. But when the whole story comes out, she clams up. She's judging me, I can tell. And now here we are, marching up Fifth Avenue, my getting fired existing silently between us. Emma is determined to ignore it, and I see nothing to do but to go along with it until she's willing to talk about this situation with Hillary.

"And here is the Empire State Building," Emma announces proudly. Seeing it up close for the first time takes my breath away. The Empire State Building is so old and…distinguished. It reminds me of my grandfather somehow. I know immediately that I love this place and it makes me love the whole city even more for taking such good care of its elders. In LA everything competes to be the newest and the brightest. I love feeling the history here seep into my pores.

I promise myself that I am going to survive this, and that I will go up to the top one day when I can enjoy the experience. But right now I have to focus on playing Frogger through the huge crowd of Japanese tourists in matching green shirts to keep up with Emma.

Every time I go into a building here, I'm forcefully reminded that I'm not in LA anymore. The air-conditioning makes every building feel like a meat locker in contrast to the humid, sunny spring heat outside.

"Listen to me, Em, you have to know I didn't throw away my entire future just to gossip. I had no idea who this guy was." I have to keep throwing it into the conversation. Because I know Emma; I know she grew up pretending nothing is wrong. Never confronting anything. And I can tell she doesn't want to start now.

At any other time I would be gawking at the incredible architecture, the way the different buildings are pushed up against each other, their competing styles meshed together to create one long city block. Emma speeds past a little café on the ground floor of a huge building, determinedly brushing past the quaint shops with ficus trees and little bistro chairs that create as much of a Parisian scene as a New Yorker can.

And then I'm totally sidetracked. "What is this?"

Emma's finally stopped at the base of some stone steps leading up to a gorgeous building with three imposing arches demanding attention.

"The New York Public Library."

"It's so beautiful," I whisper as we step inside, but

then I'm back on track. "Emma, come on, you have to believe that I wouldn't do something like this. Not on purpose." The expanse of dark woodwork, the ornate ceilings, and the upstairs balcony all serve to echo my sotto voce pleas. "Wait...I recognize this. I've seen this in movies." When I realize I know it from the original *Ghostbusters* movie, I can't help but smile. But given her mood, I'm not going to be scoring any points with Emma by bringing up my eighties obsession now.

"Oh, I'm sure. They film here all the time." She is primly moving toward the study section.

"Emma." I put all my cards out on the table, not caring how many people are shushing me at this point. "I'm going to need your help to get out of this." But Emma can't take the pressure of all the evil eyes on us. She shoots me a silent dirty look across her favorite study table. But I don't back down. She knows I will follow her around forever. Finally, she gives in to my Hillary wannabe death stare and marches back outside. But the second we're through the turnstile door, she springs her counterattack.

"Alex, you owe Hillary five million dollars. You violated your NDA." An aggressive cabbie almost veers into me as we cross the street, grabbing our attention. I can't keep up because it's just ingrained in me to stop at crosswalks before I step off a curb. A born-and-raised New Yorker, Emma seems to have no such hesitation. I look both ways at the next intersection, even though it's a one-way street, and now I'm rushing to catch up with Emma.

"I know. And it's a huge mistake. I know what I did was wrong. But I can fix this. I know I can. I just need your help."

She finally slows down on the steps of St. Patrick's Cathedral to look at me. "Alex. This is Hillary P. we're talking about. If she found out that I was talking to you, I'd be fired, too."

"She never has to know."

"Do you know how small this town is?" she shouts at me. Obviously she does not mean the teeming crowd shoving past us on Fifth Avenue. "I mean TV. The business. She finds out everything." Before I can even start to object, she gestures to me. "She found out about this."

"Emma, please."

"I'm sorry, Alex. I want to help you, I really do, but I can't afford to lose my job."

"I don't want that, either. But, come on, I can't do this alone."

"Alex, I put my neck on the line for you to get this job. You should've kept your mouth shut!" She immediately regrets saying it, I can tell. But she doesn't take it back. "Please, please don't make this harder than it is." She turns down Fifty-first Street and before I know it, she's gone.

Without anywhere to go, I see the trees of Central

Park peacefully waving in the distance and decide I need a time-out. First, I have to return to the Palace Hotel to retrieve my wheelie. Like a lifelong New Yorker, I pretended to be a hotel guest to store my kit at the bell desk so Emma wouldn't see it. It would be a distraction, seeing me pulling my makeup through the city, and I was afraid to call attention to the situation, in case she decided she had to just kick me out. I end up paying twenty bucks I can't afford, but at least I am now in possession of my makeup kit and comfortably sitting in the park on the first uninhabited bench I've found. The image of Sean jumps to the front of my mind. I'd be lying if I said it wasn't appealing. The idea of just giving up, turning this problem over to my parents. They've always been there for me. Bailing me out of one bad decision after another. This would eventually be just another funny story my dad would tell the cousins at Thanksgiving.

But I didn't come all the way to New York City to fail. I uprooted my life and moved thousands of miles across the country to succeed at the thing I truly love doing. That's why I can't let Hillary P. send me crawling back to my parents. I am not giving up.

CHAPTER SIXTEEN

After I regroup at Emma's, grateful but not sure how long I'll have access to her apartment, a quick Internet search has me on my next quest. A huge publishing building on Sixth Avenue, otherwise known as Avenue of the Americas, is home to Liz Daniels, managing editor for *Identity* magazine. I feel the massive old skyscrapers looking down on me in judgment. Trying to shake off my prevailing sense of doom, I try for a little pep talk as I handily manipulate my bulky makeup wheelie and an overnight bag I hope I won't need through the heavy revolving glass doors at the entrance.

When the security guard glances down at the clear plastic bag slung over my shoulder, revealing brushes, a dozen lipsticks, tissues, and a bulky supply of powder puffs, he waves me toward the elevators without a second thought. It's clear I have the right gear to infiltrate the fashion capital—makeup. I take a few deep calming breaths, keeping my mind on the scam I'm trying to pull rather than the crowd of businesspeople and delivery guys all jammed in around me with boxes and briefcases. Most of the people are taller than me and I use my old trick, looking up at the ceiling rather than the close shoulders boxing me in. Thankfully the crowd thins out pretty quickly and I meet no resistance from the woman at the front desk when I get off the elevator, either. Life-sized posters of *Identity* covers are on every wall. Major celebrities from the last thirty years have graced their cover. It is definitely intimidating. It took me all twenty-three floors to come up with what I thought was the perfect story to get into Liz Daniels's office. But the hungover-looking assistant saw my tools of the trade and directed me with no resistance to the editorial offices in the back. She made no move to escort me, which was probably good, because I knew this last line of defense wouldn't be so easy.

"I'm here to do Ms. Daniels's makeup?" I announce to one of the busy-looking assistants in her front office. I try to sound bored, as if it doesn't matter to me at all whether I get through those mahogany double doors or not.

"Oh, sorry. You must have the wrong day. She doesn't have any press today." The harried-looking guy with an earpiece barely looks up at me before returning his attention to his computer screen. Now, back into his mouthpiece, he says, "Sorry, yes of course, she's been waiting for Ms. Burch's call. I'll put you right through."

Thinking he's off the phone now, and relieved to

know at least Liz Daniels is in fact inside her office, I try again. "So, it's really important that I see Ms. Daniels. Um, I'm not here to do her makeup." Glancing up from nervously picking at a thread on my sweater, I realize he's not even listening to my confession. He looks engrossed in something, but from my angle I can see he's not working on his computer. "Hey. Excuse me." I wave my hand in his line of sight. He scowls at me as he pulls one ear free of his headset. Gotcha.

"What?" He smirks. "The magazine will be happy to pay your day rate if it was our mistake. Which I'm sure it wasn't. Someone will call your agency and reschedule."

"Would Liz Daniels be happy to know you're listening in on her conversations with moguls like Tory Burch?" It was a huge gamble, but it worked. And my morals apparently are taking a backseat to my survival.

"Excuse me?" He snorts in disbelief and finally gives me his attention, pulling the whole headset off his head without knocking one blond strand out of his perfectly manicured ponytail.

"You're eavesdropping on your boss. You know that could get you in a lot of trouble. Did you even read the NDA you signed?" The irony in my tone is thick, but it passes over his frosted head.

"Of course he did. Industry standard." I hear the smoke-filled, throaty New York rasp behind me and whip around to face a woman who can only be the great Liz

Daniels. She's petite, which surprises me. I was sort of picturing Meryl Streep, I think, from *The Devil Wears Prada*, but that's not this woman at all. Her deeply tanned, artificially unwrinkled skin can't contend with the creases around her lips that give away a lifetime of smoking. "Who are you?" she asks, with an intrinsic authority that makes me want to tell her my whole pathetic sob story. But that's not my plan.

"I used to work for Hillary P. I want to talk to you about the story you're doing on her." I figure if I stick as close to the truth as possible, I might attract her interest.

"Hillary?" she says slowly, and then continues to stand there in silence, sizing me up. I feel immediately uncomfortable in my casual A-line skirt and V-neck T-shirt. She is dressed in a fabulously snug black dress with a thin tortoiseshell patent leather belt at the waist, matching her tortoiseshell stilettos.

"I'm intrigued. Five minutes." She pivots with minimal movement and disappears back into her office. Obviously I don't react quickly enough, because I hear her assistant mutter, "It's only four and a half minutes now." With only a tiny jump of surprise, I'm heading after her.

Liz Daniels is standing at her windows, looking out over her cinematic view of the city. The sunlight emphasizes that she definitely doesn't need anyone to tell her how to do her makeup. It's carefully applied to seem natural and light.

"Did Hillary send you to plead on her behalf?"

"No. I'm here for me." I'd better get that said right up front. "I want you to know what a slimeball Nick Slants is. I can't imagine you would want to associate yourself or your magazine with him at all, let alone trust his voice to tell a story as scandalous as the one he's claiming about Hillary."

"I'm going to stop you right there." Liz Daniels steps around the back of her desk. "The exposé on Hillary P.'s outrageous behavior and the truth about her real personality is a huge story. I'm not going to give that up lightly. Nick Slants could be Hannibal Lecter and I'd still run the story."

"But...he's—"

"Look..." She hesitates, clearly trying to remember my name.

"Alex. Cleary," I offer.

"Let me explain something to you, Alex. You have to understand this isn't just about me running Slants's story, right? I can't not run the story. If I don't, he'll sell it somewhere else." Immediately, I see that she's right. "What's your plan? To run all over town chasing down every major editor, begging them to ignore this gold?" She holds up a thick stack of papers. "Slants may be a slimeball, but he's got a good reputation. The story is solid, sexy, and true. Hillary P. is about to fall off her self-made papier-mâché pedestal, and I personally think she deserves it. You can't protect her from this."

I STORM OUT of the publishing building on fire, and proceed to march up Sixth Avenue, my anger so apparent that even the usual crowd of oblivious pedestrians are giving me a wide berth. As the city blocks give way to the paved walking paths of Central Park, my righteous anger collapses into self-pity, and pathetically, the tears begin to stream down my cheeks as I pass by kids feeding ducks and runners circling the reservoir. I just keep walking. When I'm all cried out and the ache in my feet has pinpointed to twin blisters on my heels, I spend money I shouldn't on a cab to take me back to Times Square. I could have walked all over LA in my flip-flops, but in New York, that's what I get for wearing nice ballet flats to impress Liz Daniels. Blisters. I look around me, hating the neon lights and huge billboards. I shoot dirty looks at everyone—the colorful selfie-taking tourists as well as the bustling crowd of anonymous New Yorkers dressed in all black. As I scan the crowd, an ad with Hillary's larger-than-life face flashes on the screen above me. There she is, cooking, laughing at a guest, and then a still photo of her smiling down at me. I wonder how long it took them to Photoshop the smugness out of her expression.

But none of that matters now, does it? The self-pity routine isn't something I'm proud of, but I can't seem to help wallowing in it. Knowing those ads are on a loop, I propel myself east, away from the square, before she comes on again. New York is still so new to me, I can't help but find comfort in one of the few places that feels familiar. The heavy wooden door at TJ's opens with ease.

There's a bit of a crowd rooting for a baseball game at one end of the bar. Stupid Mets. By the time the bartender comes over I am determined to numb myself and my poor abused feet. "Two shots of tequila."

"Salt? Lime?" I shake my head. No judgment from the bartender; he doesn't even glance around looking for my companion. See, that's why you gotta love bartenders.

When he returns with the goods, I throw back both shots before he's had a chance to set out the seasoned popcorn the bar serves instead of old-school mixed nuts. No doubt my grimace is a dead giveaway that I don't normally drink like this, but I don't care. I'm considering this a special occasion.

"Okay, how 'bout a Cadillac margarita," I tell him. Not slurring my words yet. Excellent. "And some chips, *por favor.*"

He smiles. "Don't you usually get the guacamole with that?" I nod and feel embarrassingly emotional that he remembers my order. "I'll be right back," he says, and off he goes to see to it. It's weird to sit here not doing anything. Usually I would automatically reach for my phone. Check Facebook, or play a word game. Not interested. I unabashedly watch the sports fans groaning and then cheering in unison as the game continues. I count the grains on the bar. I eat the chips dipped in what passes for guacamole this far north. I slurp the margarita.

"Hey, Alex. Starting without me?" The cocktail straw flicks liquid in my face as I flinch from hearing the voice behind me.

"Billy," I say dumbly. "What are you doing here?"

"Finding you." His smile turns to an expression of concern as he looks at me more closely. "We had a date, remember?" No. Of course I don't remember that. From the moment Hillary confronted me I was only thinking about one thing. I turn back to my drink, not sure what to say, feeling a little embarrassed for Billy to see me like this. But Billy Fox doesn't just go away. He slides onto the stool next to me. "I went to the studio; you weren't there. The security guard Janeé? She thought you might be here."

"Yeah. Sorry," I mumble into my drink. It's hard not to cry on his shoulder—it's so tempting to just unload all my problems on him. I still have enough pride to keep that from happening, but small talk is beyond me at this point.

"Hey, that's okay." Billy starts to say more but stops as the bartender approaches.

"What'll it be?"

"The Macallan Twelve. Neat." Billy points to a bottle on display behind the bar. We wait silently while the bartender pours the caramel-colored liquid into a glass.

"So, you want to talk about it?" Billy finally says, taking a savoring sip.

"Not really." I sound so petulant, but I can't bring myself to care. The expression "self-destructive" comes to mind. Billy lets me wallow for a few minutes. We sip our drinks in silence. I wish my mood had affected my appetite, but I have no trouble stuffing the chips down.

When the sound of me sucking the last of my drink up the straw breaks the silence, Billy motions to the bartender for the check.

"Come on. We're getting out of here," he announces, which leads to the humbling moment where I need his help getting into my jacket.

As we step outside, the chilled evening air gets me reinvigorated a bit. I blink like I'm coming out of a daze as Billy flags down a cab easily. The ride back to his apartment goes by quicker than I'd like, as I've barely had time to mentally pull myself together.

"Here you go." I struggle to scoot myself across the backseat to get out, and Billy ends up practically lifting me bodily out of the cab.

"I can do it," I say grumpily.

"You're doing great," Billy replies, with both hands still

I guess." It's a hard admission, but now
excuses. "It seemed safe, to tell some ran-
t I hated my boss. I told him some stories
dn't even give away that I work in TV. It
me sympathy." I meet his eyes, admitting
ight on. And then it's too much.

ve been stronger." Looking out at the
m Billy's intense gaze, but the twinkling
at me, mocking my weakness. "This
aybe too tough for me."

ext to me and we are silent for a moment.
he says quietly. "But I don't think so." I
him. He's not looking out the window.
ng at me.

ver violate your trust, Billy." I want him
t. "I would never have intentionally vio-
I hope you know that."

ou. It's a tough lesson, Alex. But New
aten you yet, you know. That was just
rry. If you hang your tail between your
vay back to the warm LA beaches, then
. But if you want to try to fight for your-
surprise yourself. And *when* you win"—
l slows down to emphasize my presumed
you can do what you want."

supporting my elbow. Humoring me in the way people do when dealing with their drunken friends. The driver has brought my wheelie and overnight bag out of the trunk and sets them next to Billy, who tips him generously before hustling me and my possessions inside the building.

He keeps his eye on me as I lean against the elevator while he pulls out his key to take us to the top floor. "Have I ever mentioned how much I hate elevators? There are a lot of elevators in this city."

"Should I take your mind off it?" he asks, teasing me. But just the idea has the desired effect. My body is tingling as we stop on the top floor. Of course he lives in the penthouse. Doesn't everybody? I think, feeling snarky. An inappropriate snort of laughter bubbles up before I can stop it. His eyes widen, but Billy keeps his smile steady as he fiddles with his key ring. Bursts of giggles keep escaping as I follow him out of the elevator to an understated door off the elevator bank.

Billy efficiently escorts me inside and then collects my things while a dramatic but sincere gasp escapes me as I take in the gorgeousness. Billy, shedding the jacket accentuating his perfect physique, stands in the middle of his gorgeously appointed living space, which is designed to draw focus to the huge bay windows looking out over the park and the gorgeous sparkling city. I don't know where to look first. But obviously the skyline has captured my attention, because I don't see him coming; I just feel Billy's closeness as he gently tugs my coat off my shoulders. I smell his aftershave as he keeps his body near mine. It's like he's hoping to shelter me from what I haven't brought myself to tell him yet. It occurs to me that maybe I've been afraid to tell him because I don't know how he'll react. He's a celebrity too, though it's easy to forget when we're together. But maybe he'll be sensitive to the whole confidentiality issue and take Hillary's side. Well, now that I've identified the problem, I'm going to have to just rip the Band-Aid off. One more deep breath, drawing in his comforting warmth, and I pivot around to face him.

"Here's the thing," I say, not quite meeting his eyes. The quick turn reminds me of the alcohol that's still coursing through my system. Sitting down seems like a good idea.

"You want some coffee? Or how 'bout I get you some water?" Billy offers with Southern grace.

"No. I've got to just get this over with." Before I chicken out. "Sit," I direct. Billy evaluates me briefly, then sighs and sinks comfortably onto his sofa. With my position on the edge of the love seat, our knees are almost touching. He waits silently for me to start.

"I violated my confidentiality agreement with Hillary," I begin slowly. "I—unintentionally—talked to a reporter about her." Billy starts to speak, but now that I've started, the words rush out like a freight train. "I didn't know he

CHAPTER SEVENTEEN

～

"You're not going. Alex, be serious."

"I am being serious." I can't believe we're still arguing about this over an hour later. It's getting late on Wednesday night and I'm feeling the desperation of Friday's deadline. "You won't recognize Nick without me." It's my ace card. This is irrefutable. No matter how ridiculous it seems since the dawn of social media, Nick Slants is anonymous. His Twitter profile features a headshot of George Clooney. The photos he posts every few minutes are a dead giveaway of his location, but there are no pictures that include Nick himself. Whether Billy likes it or not, it keeps me in the game.

"Sophie will get me a picture. Being able to ID him is not a good enough reason to put yourself at risk. We'll find another way," Billy says as he disappears into the bathroom. If he thinks that's the end of this argument, he's lost his mind. The pipes whine briefly as he turns the shower on. "You know if Nick sees you there it's over, right? Alex, trust me to handle this." His deep voice carries easily through the open bathroom door. It's more than a little bit distracting knowing he's undressing on the other side of the wall. "I'll text with you the whole time, how 'bout that?" And then his voice disappears inside the fogged-up glass walls of his shower.

I know he's right about Nick. But I just feel in my gut that I have to be there tonight. It doesn't seem right to let Billy take all the risk when it's my trouble I've brought to his door. But how can I be there without Nick seeing me? Pacing a track through Billy's main living room, I'm desperately trying to work through my predicament when I trip and almost fall over the bags I left by the door. Stacking my makeup kit next to the overnight bag neatly against the wall, I am pacing back into the kitchen before it hits me.

In an instant I'm locked away in Billy's guest bathroom. Without the time to unpack and set up nicely on the roomy marble counter, I settle for just sitting on the tile in front of the floor-length mirror and getting to work.

Less than an hour later, I lean back and examine my face closely. I've done it. My huge smile completely ruins the sultry look I've created. Mental note: From now on I'm going to have to stay in character. I don't really have the right wardrobe to sell this transformation, but I'll have to make do with what I've got in my suitcase.

Pulling out the memory of high school drama class, I try to copy the posture of the girls at that calendar shoot I did, which seems like a lifetime ago now. Slinking back into the main living area, I wait for a reaction from Billy.

"Alex, there you are. Listen, there's just no way we can..." He trails off as I turn to face him. The fact that I've made him speechless should definitely go on my résumé.

"I don't think he'll recognize me now, do you?" I purr. Ha! Who knew a little makeup could give me so much confidence. Okay, a lot of makeup.

"Alex?" Billy is still shell-shocked.

"I told you I was a good makeup artist." It's hard not to be smug when he has to double-check to make sure it's still me. And frankly, I knew I could do it— I've practiced this look on several test models, though never on myself. The fact that I don't wear makeup a lot only enhances the transformation. It wasn't that hard to reshape my brows into severe manicured arches. The cat-eye look seems to change the shape of my eye with the thick, dark pencil liner I winged out and the long strip of eyelashes I glued in. I darkened my skin to a Miami Beach glowing tan color with instant tanner and lotion, and emphasized my cheekbones with a NARS crème blush called Palm Beach.

Add to that my newly ripped low-rise jeans and the form-fitting tank I've only ever worn under a blousy sweater, and I'm definitely making an impression. Unreasonably, it gives me the confidence to strut up to Billy, so close that one deep breath from either of us and our chests would touch.

"You look like a boy who knows how to party." This could be fun, I think, getting into the role by running my finger up his arm all the way to his mouth.

"Alex. It's still risky." Billy takes a deep breath and seems to force himself to pull away. "If he somehow does see through…"—he pauses, apparently searching for words, and ends up gesturing to me vaguely—"…this, it would ruin your chances of getting that story shut down."

"I know, Billy. Believe me, I know what's at stake." I follow him to look out at the spectacular view of Central Park from his penthouse window. "I also know that it's my life at stake. I can't tell you what it means to me that you want to help me. That you've come up with this incredible plan. But I can't let other people solve my problems for me for the rest of my life. I can't let you be another person who protects me from myself." Billy hears the certainty in my voice. He knows I'm not backing down. For the first time, I feel the full weight of responsibility on my own shoulders. And it feels right. It feels good. I charge forward, determined to convince Billy, too. "I'm sure about this. He won't recognize me. I won't let him. And we can sell this story together. He'll fall for it."

Billy sighs heavily. Even though we've just started dating, I know this means I've won. And when he pulls me in close, his frustration and passion are clearly evident in his kiss.

While I've been getting ready, Billy has been busy setting the stage. He shows me the tweets in the car on the way to the club. I'm not even surprised that several of Billy's celebrity friends have stepped up to help. No doubt he's done as much if not more for his friends over the years. But it's somehow both comforting and alarming to see them rallying around the plan. It is slightly relieving that Billy isn't in this alone, with only his reputation and star power at stake, but having his friends also on board heightens the twisty feeling in my gut, magnifying what's on the line if something goes wrong.

"Stop thinking so hard," Billy whispers as he pulls me out of the car onto Bleecker Street in the artsy SoHo district. The paparazzi Sophie, Billy's publicist, promised us haven't appeared yet, but since Billy had only just called her with the unusual request, it's not surprising that it didn't work. The dark street is making me nervous that this will all be for nothing. "It's going to work," Billy says with a look that for an instant makes me forget everything and appreciate the kiss he lays on me.

The kiss is electric. An instant after his lips connect with mine, his arms strongly drawing me flush up against him, and I'm lost in the moment. It takes several moments for me to register that even with my eyes closed, they are flinching from the blindingly bright flashes from several different cameras all crowding around us. The paparazzi appeared out of nowhere. Obviously Sophie Atwater has a way of getting things done for her clients.

"All right, guys." Billy laughs good-naturedly. "At least let us go get a drink." He ushers me past the photographers, who are all racing to be the first to get the new photos uploaded. I don't even recognize some of the technology they sync up with their long-lens cameras, but I have no doubt I'm going to see it all online in minutes.

Which for once is exactly what we're counting on.

Billy speaks with the manager of the loud dance club, and he settles us into a large corner booth in a private area. He brings over the drinks menu, which just about makes my eyes pop out of my head.

"A thousand dollars for a vodka?"

"It's for the whole table," Billy says, as if that explains anything. "Is that what you want?"

"No, no. I'm fine. Thanks," I say, scanning the list to see that everything on the menu has the same outrageous prices.

"Well, we have to get something." He never even picks up the list; he just gestures to the waiter I didn't notice hovering nearby. "Let's have some Scotch. Do you still have a bottle of that Glenfiddich 25 somewhere?" The waiter looks mildly dazed at the request.

"We'll have that, and I think the ladies would like the vodka service." After the waiter heads off to fulfill our outrageously expensive orders, the humor leaves Billy's face, and he goes very still as he catches me still staring at him. "We're putting on a show here, right? You know this isn't my life anymore."

"I know," I reply simply. It's a bit unsettling how comfortable he is with all this.

"I don't need this." Billy gestures around us. "I just want to be sure we're clear on that. This is my past. And this." His hand flicks between us.

"We are not having this conversation right now," I interrupt, grabbing his hand to stop him. But I end up pulling him closer to me. "You're taking a big risk for me. We need to concentrate on what we're doing."

"Doesn't mean we can't have some fun in the process." And that's all the warning I get before he pulls me onto his lap and kisses me so deeply it's hard to remember we're still in full view of everyone in the darkly lit dance club.

After an hour, Billy's private table is filled with celebrities and even a few significant others. I'm starting to sweat from the dancing we've done. Billy took me out first, but then his friend Jared asked me to dance, and a few of the girls in the group and I had to honor the Madonna mash-up the DJ played. But I'm still sipping my first cocktail and my eyes never stop scanning the crowd, looking for Nick's slimy self to appear.

Finally, returning from a trip to the bathroom, which took longer than usual because I had to reglue my false eyelashes, I see Slants hunched over his drink at the bar. He's clearly scanning the room, as most single men in the club are doing. But it's clear that his eyes keep resting too long on the celebrity party in the corner.

I slip back into the VIP section, showing my hand stamp to the badass guy whose sole job is preventing enthusiastic fans from interrupting Billy and his friends' evening.

Snuggling in between Billy and Jared, I make sure not to even glance in the direction of the bar as I announce, "He's here. At the bar."

With no hesitation Billy meets eyes with a few of the others in the group. "Okay, guys, this is it." The tone of our group goes immediately from vibrant and raucous to more intimate and quieter, which syncs up perfectly with the plan. We're all huddled up, and without glancing away from our intimate discussion, I can tell our new vibe has been noticed not just by the fans and partiers on the floor but by the sleazeball at the bar, too.

"I guess this is my cue to bow out." Bailey, the youngest of the group, draws our attention. I was surprised when she joined us, since her image isn't exactly one that would fit in with what we had planned. Bailey is one of those former Disney singer/actresses that has managed to keep her clean-cut, wholesome image even into her twenties. Her cute brunette pixie cut is sassy and sweet at the same time.

She looks at Billy awkwardly. "I only took one course in stage fighting."

Billy's smirk is dark and almost unkind, but his low voice is the opposite. "It's okay, B. Just sell it." He prompts her into action by obviously moving his hand onto her thigh. She lurches away and smacks him hard across the cheek. I am so stunned, for a second I gasp, not knowing how to react.

"To hell with this," she spits at us, and storms off, clearly muttering under her breath. I stare at her, shocked, as she passes the bar, and my eyes lock with Nick's fascinated gaze. Luckily Jared stands up, breaking our eye contact before I can do anything to blow my cover. Billy pulls me to stand, and with his hand possessively on my backside leans in and says, "I think act one went very well." As he pulls us toward the door, I realize many in the club failed to notice the celebrity drama unfolding. The bass line is still thumping out a dance rhythm. But the one person we wanted interested is clearly on the hook. I am being shoved quickly past Nick, and I do my best to be confident in my disguise. Fingers crossed he didn't recognize me.

Once through the doors, we pile into Jared's limo to regroup. Billy looks questioningly at Jared.

"Well, I got my line out in time." It's as if we're talking about some sort of wacky improv theater show. "He definitely heard me say 'Lion's Den.' But I didn't want to oversell it, so I don't know what else he heard."

"That's fine. That's great. If he didn't catch on, maybe we can tweet a picture that gives away where we are. I'd rather not, you know, get too many real fans there, if we can help it. But if he doesn't follow that's our backup."

"How great was Bailey?"

I can't help but feel out of the loop as Jared and Selma break down the details of the slap.

"That had to sting, Bill."

"She was aiming to just land it with her fingers. But I think we misjudged a bit," Billy says ruefully, rubbing his jaw.

"Why? Why did she storm out?" I finally have to ask.

"Well, when she offered to help, we agreed her Disney-kid image is too pristine for even Nick to believe she'd get into something this dark, so we figured we'd play on that."

"I tried to talk her into dropping an F-bomb on the way out." Selma laughs. "Let's see if she did." She pulls out her phone and starts typing.

"Alex, we're dropping you off at the apartment. Selma? Where should we drop you, honey?"

"Do you have time to stop by my hotel? I'm in Midtown. Near Thirty Rock."

"Oh, doing the *Today* show tomorrow?" Jared asks.

"Yeah, the eight o'clock hour. I have a five a.m. makeup call. This was so fun, I'm going to crash as soon as I get to my room." She's already snuggling up in her side seat of the limo.

"Don't forget to wash your face." I can't help it. The advice comes out automatically before I can stop myself. Too many actresses just let it sit on their skin all night; it's so bad for the skin, not to mention gross.

"I know you're right." She sighs, closing her eyes. I love that she isn't even offended or surprised by my comment. That's the world of an actress, I guess. They're used to it. "I didn't bring my cleanser, though. Maybe the hotel will have some."

The limo pulls up in front of Billy's apartment building. "Wait here a second," I say to Billy. "You have time, right?"

"Oh, sure." He smiles warmly at me. "We don't want to get there too soon. Let Nick sweat for a minute."

I dash into the building and use Billy's key to take me directly to the top floor. Once inside I tear apart my kit quickly but carefully, putting together a little care package before heading back downstairs.

"Here," I say through the window, handing Selma the small makeup bag. "A facial cleanser and some of my favorite lotion. Promise me you'll use it," I say with authority.

"Okay, okay, you're right. My makeup artist will love you tomorrow." She takes the bag and looks inside. "Oh, it smells amazing. Thank you, Alex."

"Thank you so much for helping me," I reply. "It's the least I can do."

"All right, kiddo, let's get you to bed," Billy says to Selma as she shuts her eyes, still holding my care package. He takes my hand, which is still resting against the open window. "You scan social media, keep me posted on his movements and anything that jumps out at you, okay?"

"Yes. Okay," I say, determined to do my part, hating that he's going to be out there so publicly risking his neck for me.

"It's going to work out. Slants will learn a lesson he won't soon forget." He uses his grip on my hand to pull my upper body into the car for one more unforgettable kiss. I slowly find my balance to stand up and watch the limo pull back out into the night. Billy Fox is just too good to be true.

SITTING IN BILLY'S apartment waiting for something to happen is torture. It's like sitting on the set of the slowest film shoot ever, waiting for the actors to finally spit out their lines correctly. I hit refresh on Twitter and Facebook, and then check my watch obsessively for half an hour with no new posts or updates from Nick or Billy. I search the hashtag #LionsDen and their Twitter as well as running a Google search on both the club and Nick Slants to see if there's any news I'm missing. Still nothing.

> **Me:** just checking in. are you at the club yet?

I can't help it. I send the text to Billy knowing full well he'd text me if there was anything to share. But I still stare at the screen, willing it to light up with his response. And then it does.

> **Billy:** just walked in. perfect timing. He's already here.
> **Billy:** huddled in a corner
> **Me:** amazing. Okay. I'll let you know when he posts something.

Billy's fridge is stocked with drinks: sodas, several different types of waters, beer, and mixers. I look around his kitchen—maybe he has a second refrigerator for food? But no, clearly Billy Fox does very little cooking. The kitchen has gorgeous dark granite countertops that look like nothing more than a cup of coffee has ever sat on them. I do find cereal when I open a cupboard—just looking for the glasses, of course. Pops, Cocoa Puffs, and raisin bran.

Deciding to stick with the filtered water from the fridge, I'm back at my workstation when the apartment phone rings. I freeze, feeling like a criminal as a few rings echo through the open floor plan. After Billy's brief outgoing message, a female voice carries loudly. "Hello? Alex? Pick up if you're there." There's a brief pause as

I wrap my head around the fact that the voice leaving the message is calling out to me. How does she know I'm here? I'm not sure if I should answer, until she tries again. "Alex, it's Sophie Atwater. Billy's publicist. Please pick up." Another impatient silence as I dash to the desk, searching for an extension.

"Hello? This is Alex." The disorienting sound of my own voice on speaker ends abruptly, so I clear my throat and parrot, "This is Alex."

"Oh, good. Alex, we need to talk about this absurd plan."

I don't know what she expects me to say to that. So I hold my ground by remaining silent. I can tell the line is alive; there's a bit of sound in the background from her side. Like maybe she's closing a door. It's starting to feel ridiculous, this phone standoff. And then I hear her sigh heavily.

"Look, Alex. Billy explained what's at stake for you, and I get it. Whether you believe this or not, I'm trying to help you. I sent paparazzi to that damn club, for God's sake." I wait…there's clearly a "but" coming. "But," Ah ha! "I think it's also a very bad idea for Billy to jeopardize his entire career to help you."

"I don't want that, either. This plan isn't my idea." Sounding defensive is probably not the strongest position, but I can't help it.

"No, I get it. Once Billy has an idea in his head…

well, let's just say he has a lot in common with steam-rollers."

"I've noticed."

"So where are we with this? Am I going to be putting out fires all over town tomorrow?"

"I hope not. The plan is for Nick to want to hold on to this story—reveal it himself. He's all about getting credit for the scoop, you told Billy that yourself." I remind her this scheme was practically her idea.

Clearly Sophie is not falling for that tactic. "Oh, no question, Nick Slants's motives are less than subtle. I've had any number of run-ins with him over the years, and I'm sure you have a fairly clear idea of what his next move will be."

"Well, good. Then this should all work out and everyone will be fine and Slants will get what he deserves."

"Do you realize how insanely overconfident you both are about this? I've devoted my career to managing relationships between celebrities and reporters of all levels. And with almost twenty years of practical experience, I would never put someone else's reputation on the line for myself. And here you just met Billy, what? A month ago? And all of a sudden he's risking everything for you? And you're letting him?" I listen to her carry on, thinking a couple of things. One, no wonder she's good at her job. When she's passionate about something, she's clearly very persuasive. And two, she's right. That is what's turning my stomach inside out as I sit there and force myself to listen to every word Sophie Atwater has to say until she finally runs out of steam.

"You'd better still be there," she finally says into the silence.

"I'm here," I reply. "I just...don't know what to say. You're right." I wipe my hand over my face and when it comes away with smudges of red lipstick and black mascara, I realize I'm still all made up in my disguise from earlier. "I don't want this to backfire on Billy, either."

"Then stop him," she commands. I can feel the intensity of her personality through the phone.

"Oh God. Okay. I'll try." I grab my phone off the counter and open it to the messaging page, only to see that a number of texts from Billy have come in while I wasn't looking. "He's been texting me while I was talking to you."

"What'd he say?"

"He's asking me to check Twitter."

"I'm on it—I haven't seen anything. Keep reading."

"He thinks he's done it. He had Jared with him."

"Right, I know—not sure how I'm going to explain this to Jared's publicist."

"Well, he and Jared are pretty sure Slants overheard them talking about the party."

"Damn it. Here it is," I hear on the other end of the line. "Nick has posted on his Twitter and Facebook accounts that he's about to break some huge news. That it will 'rock the entertainment industry to its foundation.' Hyperbole much?" she critiques as she reads. I don't know how she can even speak. I'm shaking so hard I have to sit down. I lean against the cupboards in the kitchen, staring sightlessly at the highly polished tile flooring.

The sound of her typing is the only thing I hear for at least a minute. "Alex? Are you still there?" she asks after a while. I don't know why, but I've still got the phone pressed to my ear so hard it stings. "Alex?"

"Yeah. I'm here."

"What's done is done." She sighs heavily. "Billy may be a pigheaded romantic fool, but he's our fool. Am I right?" All of a sudden, she has a completely out-of-context resigned lightheartedness to her tone.

"What are you talking about?"

"Well, I couldn't stop it, which would have been my first choice. Now I'm gonna have to spin it."

"I don't understand what you mean. Spin what?" I lower my voice as I hear Billy come in the front door.

"Oh, no way..." he says as he comes to crouch beside me. "Sophie thinks she's gonna get the spin machine working on this?"

"Damn it, Billy! I'm not your fairy godmother, you know!" Sophie shrieks so loudly my self-preservation kicks in and I hold the phone away from my ear. Billy leans in closer, his eyes still on mine, and speaks into it.

"It's gonna work, Sophie. You know it is. Now stop spooking my girl, here." He strokes my hair as if I'm a scared filly and he is the horse whisperer. "We'll talk in the morning."

"You're damn straight we will. I'm upping my rate for this month. Do you realize what favors I'm going to have to pull to get you out of this?!"

"I don't want you to get me out of anything. Just let me lead Nick Slants exactly where he wants to go. We are going to get Alex out of this hot water." A loud silence. "Sophie, I'm serious. Do not pull one of your magic acts and make this all disappear. I've set it up perfectly." He gently takes the phone from me and stands up, swiftly turning away from me. "I'm not kidding about this, Sophie, and don't pretend you don't know what I'm talking about. I know all about how you squashed that story of Louise Chase's face-lift last month." Now I really wish I could hear the other half of this conversation. "Yes, I do. And that's not going to happen. This is going public and you're going to let it." There's a beat as he listens. I see every muscle in his back tighten under his light knit navy blue Henley.

"You're not going to regret it. When have I ever let you down?" The charming Southern drawl in his voice tells me he's gotten his way, as he clearly always does. But then he turns back to me with a concerned look. "She wants to talk to you again." But he stays in place. Since when am I a mouse timidly hiding out on the floor? I get to my feet and reach for the phone.

"It's me," I say, once again in possession.

"Well, he's definitely determined to see this through." She sighs again.

"I'm not going to let anything go wrong. I know it's a risk. And I know how lucky I am that he is willing to help me, because no one else on the planet would have. But it'll be worth it."

CHAPTER EIGHTEEN

From the moment I woke up Thursday morning I could not shake the sense of impending doom that sat on my chest. So far everything was going according to plan. Nick Slants posted on Twitter and his Facebook page that he was working on a major story. Something that would blow everyone's minds. So far the items have been "blind"—there were hints that could have referred to Billy, but they were vague enough that only we knew what he meant.

Although Sophie announced that she's reserving the right to say "I told you so" if our plan backfires, she has thrown herself into the effort to make sure it doesn't. And despite it stemming more from a "if you can't beat 'em, join 'em" mentality, I appreciate her help nonetheless.

Sophie's been sending us links and headlines every time Nick's big announcement gets picked up by another media outlet. So far, it hasn't made the mainstream press. "This isn't good enough." Billy paces back and forth in front of the huge picture windows framing his Manhattan city view. "We have to get him to make this bigger."

"You know there's only one way to do that," I say.

"We're not putting you in his path, Alex. And that's final." He glares at me as he lifts up my bare feet from the coffee table to slide past and sit next to me on the sofa. Billy hasn't changed out of his workout clothes, but even in his sweaty, ratty gym gear, he's still the most handsome man I've ever seen. "You're just being stubborn. Nick Slants is a jerk, but he's not going to physically hurt me."

Billy puts his sneakers up on the coffee table, stretching way past my dark-blue-polished toes. "I don't like the idea of him getting near you again. Who knows what that guy is capable of?"

"Okay, fine. I won't be alone with him. But you have to admit this is the best way to up the stakes and get Nick to go prime time with his news." I meet his eyes and let him see my determination to see this through. "Billy, you're in this mess because of me. I need to be a part of making things right. How can I face myself in the mirror again if I let you fight my battles for me?"

He stares at me for a long minute before finally accepting that I'm not going to give up on this. "All right, let me talk to Sophie and see if there's any shows in the NBC studios she can book me on tonight."

"I'll get my kit ready," I say without hesitating. I don't want to give Billy time to change his mind. I head to the guest bedroom to pack up everything from last night's glamorous makeup disguise.

BEFORE I KNOW IT, I'm back in the building where I was fired and humiliated yesterday. It seems crazy to be here again, but the fact that it's the same building Hillary works in is just a side note. Giving my driver's license to the security guard, I force a smile as they take a picture for my day badge. It's a terrible picture, but it allows me access to the green room at the *Late Night* show.

I got here early, wanting a chance to set up before Jared and Billy arrive. With all that's going on, it's true, I'm actually nervous to do Billy's makeup for the show. Guys in general and certainly guys with good skin like Billy wear just a tiny bit of powder. But still, there's a finesse to doing it correctly that everyone learns in beauty school. Looking at the monitor and seeing that Billy looks like he has makeup on would definitely make it onto my top ten worst possible scenarios.

I check in with the NBC page in the green room. She shows me to the private dressing room she assigned to Billy and Jared. Usually they'd get their own rooms, but it's a full show tonight, she explains, and since they're in a skit together she was hoping that would be okay. I assure her I think they'll be fine about it.

While waiting for the guys to arrive, I try to act casual,

hanging out in the green room. Celebs and up-and-coming talent come and go, their reps grabbing heaping plates from the cheese and fruit trays. There are plenty of sodas and like nine different types of water. I choose a plain Fiji from the selection and even try to subtly photobomb the guest band's behind-the-scenes selfie they're talking about posting. It would be ideal if Nick Slants sought me out, but if he doesn't know I'm here, why would he?

This is the first time I've wished I'd started a public profile the way so many hair and makeup artists have. JLo's stylist did a workshop at my beauty school and she explained it's about giving out free tips and insider scoop on products, and if you post a few pictures with your celebrity, it helps build your numbers. But why do I need followers? It just never seemed to make sense to me. Until now. If this whole experience is teaching me anything, it's that when opportunity knocks, you'd better answer.

Jared gets there before Billy. I want to make sure Jared isn't uncomfortable with me, so I do my put-them-at-ease routine involving self-deprecating jokes and an up-front agreement that if there's anything he doesn't like, he only has to say so; there's no ego with me.

Things go pretty fast. Jared, like Billy, has nice clean skin, but I pull out my clippers to clean up the back of his neck and his sideburns. I'm styling his hair in the spiky way he's known for when Billy joins us in the dressing room.

"Sorry I'm late. There was a bigger group of fans out front than usual. Must be spring break!"

"I should've waited for you. The fans would've gotten the word out that we're here tonight faster than anything."

"We'll post a picture in the green room anyway. We need to do it in time for Nick to get down here."

"He's always lurking in this part of town. Maybe because so many studios are here—celebs pass through here all the time." I add, "Remember, he was at the bar two blocks over every night around this time. He'll be close by." I clean my brushes while the guys switch seats. I tuck a few tissues into the collar of Billy's blue button-down shirt. It matches his eyes perfectly and it's hard not to get distracted.

I get through Billy's makeup quickly, and he's just taken the brush from me to fix his hair himself when the page knocks on the door and opens it before the words "come in" have been announced.

"Oh!" It's more a breath than an exclamation. The page turns a charming beet red, clashing horribly with her maroon uniform. I can't help but feel for her—even working at *Late Night*, she's not immune to Jared and Billy together. It's a pretty impressive display.

"Yes? Madison?" Luckily saying her name shakes her out of her stupor.

"Oh, yes." She giggles at me, and I smile back, commiserating. "You're Alex, right? Someone's waiting for you at downstairs security. Did you have a guest coming here today?"

My eyes dart to Billy's. He gives a tiny nod.

"Yes, actually. I did have a friend coming by. Is that a problem? He can wait downstairs..."

"Oh, I'm sure we can get him cleared for the green room. I mean, you're here with Billy Fox, after all."

"Thanks. It's Madison, right?" Billy doesn't even have to try for charming her, a hint of his Texas drawl doing the work for him.

"Yes, of course. Come with me, Alex. I'll show you where to sign your friend in."

We go through corridors that all seem identical. I'd be so lost if I hadn't spent months working on a set that is the mirror image of this one. Quickly, I'm back out in the front lobby looking for the smug, sleazy face of Nick Slants. But he's not one of the several people waiting amid the modern furniture in the corner of the huge building. I look around, my brows drawn together in consternation. Where could Nick have gone?

"I kept waiting for you to text me." The flat California accent stands out amid the New York–based crew.

"Sean!" I try to plaster a happy-to-see-you look of welcome on my face. "Sean! I'm so sorry, I've been so slammed."

"Alex, I should have said this two days ago. I don't blame you for not texting me; I wasn't being straight with you." A fresh load of guilt washes over me as he puts his hands on my shoulders and pulls me in close to him. "I came to New York to see you. I miss you," he whispers quietly.

"Sean…" There are a million things running around in my mind. I want to comfort him, tell him I miss him, too. I want to kick his shin and tell him to beat it, remind him he's the one who broke up with me. But all of that is taking a backseat to the fact that Nick Slants could show up at any minute and I need to be ready to throw the lure.

"No, wait. Let me talk first." Sean looks around the huge lobby area and pulls me toward some aerodynamic, minimalist, pristine white seating arrangement that a small group of Japanese tourists are awkwardly perched on.

"Sean, this really isn't a good time for me." I pull myself out of his gentle grasp before he has me seated next to the brightly dressed guests waiting for an escort.

"I know—you're working. And listen, Alex…" He puts his hands on my shoulders, looking me in the eyes. "I'm impressed. You've proven your point." He steps back to gesture to the massive, bustling lobby. "You've shown me, your family, everyone that you can make it here in the big city. And you were right. We all underestimated you."

It's not what I expected him to say. Sean was never one for admitting he was wrong. I can't help but soften a bit toward him for doing it now.

"Thank you, Sean. It means a lot to hear you say that."

"Well, you deserve it...all your hard work, and look where you are. You're a success!" He looks around the marble-and-glass lobby, clearly impressed. Any good feelings just withered away into a tiny hypocritical ball. My only success to date is creating a debacle that I have a snowball's chance in hell of getting out of. Especially if I sit here, chatting with Sean, instead of getting myself into the vicinity of Nick Slants.

"Come home, Alex." Sean puts his hand on my cheek, bringing my eyes back to his fierce gray ones. "You've made your point. But you can work in LA." My mind freezes on the words "you made your point." What is *that* supposed to mean? But he keeps talking. "Your family misses you. I miss you."

"Sean, I wasn't just making a point. I'm making a career for myself," I clarify with steely intention.

"Right, of course. That's what I mean." Sean recovers quickly. "Alex, I get it now. This is important to you. And that's fine. But couldn't you try to do it back home? I want us to try again. I want you to give me another chance."

I look away from his impassioned, sincere face. Am I supposed to believe he's totally seen the light? Out of the blue? Right when I decide to interrupt him and put an end to this charade, I see Nick Slants walking through the revolving glass doors. He makes a beeline for me.

"Alex, are you listening? I get it now. And I want the

same things you do. So let's do it. What do you say?" He's still got my hand in his.

"Sean, wait a second." I tug on my hand, but he doesn't let go. My eyes dart to Nick, who is now hanging back, watching us like we're his favorite soap opera. "Sean. Just hold on. What are you saying?" I know I should just get rid of him, but I can't help asking the question.

"Isn't it obvious? Alex, I want us to get married. I was an idiot to let you get away. And I want to fix it. I promise. Come home, and we'll make everything right." I can feel Nick's eyes bouncing back and forth between us and it's making me sick to my stomach.

"I have to go back to work, Sean. I can't talk about this now."

"Of course. I understand." He says the words, but the frustration in his voice is hard to miss. "Just promise me you'll think about it. I'm not going home until we talk about this."

"Okay," I say, wishing I had the time to resolve this now. Sean is *staying* in Manhattan? "I'll call you. As soon as I can." Before I can fully step back, Sean leans in and kisses me firmly on the lips. And then he turns and walks out. Right past our audience of one. Nick saunters up to me and disgustingly begins a golf clap.

"How romantic. You'll have to tell me how it ends."

"Nick?! What the hell are you doing here?" I delay, trying to get myself back on track.

"Well, I could ask you the same thing. But I'm glad you're here. I need your help."

"Why in God's name would I help you?" I'd put my death stare up against Hillary's anytime.

"What's happened? You're angry?" Nick asks in a cocky voice, but it's undercut by how compulsively he keeps checking his phone.

"Yeah, I think I have the right to be pretty angry. You tricked me into confiding in you about things, and then used me as your 'source.'" Nick's eyes widen as my words start to sink in. "You got me fired, Nick. I wouldn't pour water on you if you were on fire after what you did. So get lost." Running the biggest bluff of my life, I turn my back on him. Ignoring my churning stomach and pounding heart, I force myself to walk toward the elevator bank. He's still back there. I can practically hear him thinking, hopefully trying to work his next angle. My heart is already slamming double time. I don't know if I will make it up to the *Late Night* studios floor without losing my lunch, but I just keep putting one foot in front of the other. This has to work.

"Look, Alex, I'm sorry it all came down the way it did." Nick oozes sincerity as he catches up with me before I clear the security turnstile. "I meant to tell you who I was, but you gave me those quotes...And let me tell you, after what Hillary's done to so many people in this industry? The damage she's caused? You did the right thing speaking out."

"I didn't 'speak out.'" I have to force every word past my locked jaw. "You tricked me. I would never have said those things on the record. And now you're acting as if you're out for the greater good? Spare me."

"Fine. How 'bout this? I'll take your name out of it. Hillary may have fired you, but if I change it to 'insider source' you might still be able to work in Hollywood."

I look at him suspiciously. "Why would you do that?"

"Okay, here's the thing…Alex." Nick takes a deep breath. "I've caught on to this huge…thing. A story. That could be huge. Like, bigger than Brad and Angelina. It's like if Bill Cosby and Heidi Fleiss had a scandal baby." I gasp at his grossly callous assessment, but he continues, oblivious. "This thing could explode. I don't even know how many A-listers are involved. But it's happening like now. Tonight. And you can help me get into the scene."

"And if I help you, you'll take my name out of the article?" I reiterate slowly, really letting it sink in.

"More than that…If you want me to keep your name off that article, we have to go now."

I'd rather swallow nails than go anywhere with this dirtbag, but I remind myself my entire career, my pride, literally everything I have is at stake here. This is my only option.

"What would I have to do?"

He hears the reluctance, the lack of trust in my voice, and dials up the charm. "Okay. Last night I managed to sneak into the after-party of a premiere event on the West Side. There were a bunch of A-list celebs there. I couldn't really get photos, it was so dark, but I overheard a few conversations and managed to put together that there is some ugly shit going on right now."

"Ugly?"

"Yeah. Some of the guys were talking in code about an invitation-only poker game. But then when I was staking out the bathroom…" I can't contain my eye roll at that, which of course Nick defends. "Dude, Alex, you wouldn't believe the stuff guys say at the urinals." I just shake my head, trying to clear the disgusting visual from my mind as Nick glances at his watch and then continues enthusiastically. "Anyway, in walk two major stars. I recognize both their voices. And they are…legit."

"Who?" Because it would look weird if I didn't ask.

"It was…" Nick hesitates, looking around to make sure he's not overheard. "I'm not sure I'm ready to share that information with you yet. And anyway, it doesn't matter. The point is these two guys were talking about this 'poker game' but, like, using air quotes. It's totally a code for something else. And what I could tell from what they were saying, it's like—I think it's…"—I can practically hear the drumroll in his head—"an illegal sex ring. Probably tons of drugs…" Nick trails off, as if it's manna from the gods. He's probably imagining the headlines right now.

I bring him back to earth. "Nick, that's not a story.

Who cares if celebs are having sex? And everyone assumes they're doing some sort of drugs, right? That's Hollywood. I don't think that's going to be headline news."

"You have no idea. This goes so much deeper. I'm not just talking sex. They were talking about any kind of sex you could want. With a sex ring—who knows? Kinky stuff? Minors? Prostitutes? Sex slaves? Human trafficking? I might get a Peabody for this. Oh my God. I bet they're doing stuff that makes Charlie Sheen look like an amateur."

I snort my disbelief.

"Exactly—me saying it isn't enough. That's why you have to get me upstairs. Like, now." I look at my security pass, then back up at him. "It's worth it. This is the story of the century. And I'm going to be the face of it." He sees my distress and goes in for the kill. "I'll make it worth your while. After this, I could charge double for the Hillary story...everyone will want my byline. But, like I said, I'll take your quotes out of it." He pats my shoulder, full of assurances. "I promise."

"What studio are we going to?" He can't help but smirk at the hint of me caving in.

"The *Late Night* show's green room. Hillary P.'s stage is just down the hall, right?"

"You got me fired, Nick. Now you want me to just waltz in there with a guest?"

"For God's sake, Alex. Can you get me in or not?

I've got other connections if you can't do it, and then our deal is off. I'll run the article about Hillary, and with the publicity I'll have from this epic story, you'll be the most famous whistle-blower since Monica Lewinsky." The scope of this is so intimidating. But I can't chicken out now. I pull out my ID card with a deep breath and head over to the security desk.

The afternoon guard shift is run by a fabulous diva named Janeé. She always wears full-glam eye makeup and bright red lips that contrast spectacularly with her dark skin. We bonded my second day when I gave her a new lip pencil that has a long-lasting no-smear promise on the packaging. I knew the color was something Hillary couldn't wear, but would be perfect for Janeé.

"Hey, Janeé. What's up?" That's me, super casual. You never know what mode she'll be in, and since she's almost six feet tall, definitely over two hundred pounds, you don't want to get on Janeé's bad side. Ever.

"Alex. What's up, girl?" Janeé gives Nick the full head-to-toe inspection. "I got to say, I like the other one better." Nick darts me an angry look and pointedly pulls out his watch again.

"I know. Me too," I say, moving up to Janeé's counter so Nick is behind me. "But I left something of his upstairs. Could you just let me bring him up for a minute?"

"Honey, you know you're not on the list anymore. Your card should've been confiscated," she says loudly, clearly for Nick's benefit. With my back blocking my movement, I quickly shove my day pass for *Late Night* across the table at her. Let Nick think I'm bribing her.

"It'll only take me a second, Janeé. I promise. It's personal stuff, you know? Nick's cool. He's just with me for moral support," I beg shamelessly.

Janeé takes her time sizing Nick up again, and I can feel him starting to sweat, which I can't help but enjoy. Then she raises a darkly lined eyebrow at me and smirks. "Okay, honey. But make it quick. And don't let your friend touch anything."

"Right, you got it." As Nick is practically dragging me toward the turnstile into the elevator bank, I shoot back, "You're the best, Janeé, thank you!"

HAVING SAFELY MADE IT to the elevator bank, Nick presses the up arrow. He keeps nervously checking our backs as if at any second Janeé is going to come tearing around the corner and bodily force our removal.

"What's the plan, once we get there?" I ask as we step on board. Miraculously, the large corporate elevator is empty except us, so I give myself plenty of space opposite him. I wonder how much of this he's going to tell me. Watching the floors tick by, I'm running out of time. "What are you doing?" I bug him again as he checks his phone. "Posting about this?" So much for subtlety.

"Yes, as a matter of fact, I am," he says smugly. "I'm building anticipation for my big news."

"What, to your eight thousand Twitter followers?" I taunt.

"It just starts there. It'll go viral, don't worry." Worry? Ha. He doesn't know the half of it.

"But then it's not your story, is it? People will forget all about who discovered something this shocking, right? CNN, NBC, they'll all have their own reporters on it and you'll be nothing." He ignores me and keeps flipping through his phone, but my gut is telling me I've gotten to him. I can afford to hold out a few more floors, make him come to me.

"So, what? How do I keep my name attached?" he says casually, but I can see the intensity behind his eyes. I hope it's enough.

"Well, I don't know..." I pause as if thinking it through. "You shouldn't just write something other people can copy and paste. You have to be on camera. Yourself, you know?"

"No one knows what I look like. I've kept it a mystery. People speculate all the time," Nick says, clearly proud of his little game. "You wouldn't believe how much easier it is to get the scoop anonymously."

"That comes as no surprise to me." And I let the silence sit for a second. "But maybe that's why you do it. You out yourself, going *live* or something. Because you have to reveal this corruption. It just adds to the story." And then I shut up. I want to pump him up, not get so dramatic he becomes suspicious.

"Yeah, I don't know if I can make something like that happen that fast."

"No, you're probably right. Would you need a full-on, live satellite truck?" I muse. "Or maybe you just use Skype. Or not. But what the hell, it would've been great, right? Everyone saying your name?" Oh, the timing couldn't have been better. The elevator doors open and we're at the thirty-seventh floor and now this Hail Mary scheme is all hinging on Nick's ego.

CHAPTER NINETEEN

Watching Nick Slants sitting in the corner of the green room eavesdropping on Billy makes me sick to my stomach. He made me stand with him at first. "Act natural," he said "and no one will question us." I shot him a disbelieving look as we passed by Billy, and Nick responded with snide remarks about my run-in with Sean downstairs, knowing I couldn't respond the way I wanted to without drawing attention to us. I finally just walked off under the guise of gathering up a plate from the gorgeous snack spread. So now cheese, fruits, and gourmet little sandwiches are all stuffed on my small plate, but I can't force a bite down.

I'm lurking in the corner when all of a sudden I panic—my makeup set bag will be a dead giveaway to Nick that I'm legitimately here working. He'll put me together with Billy and blow the whole plan. I glance around subtly, trying to figure out where I put it down before I went downstairs and ran into Sean. The show starts playing on the screen. The opening monologue and accompanying band completely drown out Billy's fake phone calls, but I know he's working the plan.

Billy slams his fist into the arm of the chair and I jump in reaction. Almost losing the avocado off my plate, I have to concentrate on not making a mess for a second and I miss Nick's reaction. A bomb could go off and Nick wouldn't notice, he's so engrossed in the angry details Billy is feeding him.

"I hate to interrupt, Mr. Fox, but the stage managers asked for you to go get your mic on. You'll be on in a minute." An incredibly young intern interrupts Billy and then scurries off just as quickly.

"Great. Just perfect." Billy grunts. He rises to his feet and heads toward the stage. My makeup bag is right next to his chair. I glance around, hoping no one calls attention to it.

"Did you get what you need?" I ask Nick casually as he quickly starts to load up a plate. I thought he would leave right away. He's eating? Now?!

"Can you pack this up for me to go?" He shoves a roast beef sandwich at me before I can answer. "I'm meeting a crew downstairs. I think I can break this live on my website. My IT guy is building me a platform now."

Amazingly, his ego has him convinced this was his idea. Even better. I close up the box of food and without glancing back at my makeup kit or to where Billy's headed backstage, I insist, "I'm escorting you back out of the building." The suspicion in my voice is not feigned.

The cat-that-ate-the-canary grin on Nick's face is so disgustingly sleazy. My fingers are itching to slap it off his smug face as we ride down in the elevator. It's only when he's gone back into the public lobby and I'm on my way back up that I realize either my violent disgust toward Nick or my protective feelings toward Billy kept me from feeling closed in on the elevator ride. Normally it would have been hard for me to catch a breath without my mental exercises, but today, I was too busy seething to even notice.

"BILLY, I CAN'T thank you enough for what you're doing for me. Really. You are amazing. And I'm so grateful." Something changes behind his eyes as I am quickly applying a rice-paper blotting tissue across his forehead before he goes on camera.

"You're welcome," he says quietly, watching the backstage monitor. We're near the sound guy, who is still futzing with his mic.

"Wait, did I say something wrong?" I whisper, confused by his distance. And I scoot out of the way to let the already annoyed audio guy get in to clip the mic to the front of Billy's shirt.

"It's nothing. I've got to concentrate now." There is an

unwritten code about disrupting performers before they go on. Actually, it probably is written down somewhere. And I would never, ever want to upset Billy, or any performer, before he had to get out there in front of an audience.

"You're good." The sound man waves him off with a thumbs-up.

When Billy tries to step past, I am just as surprised as he is that I've moved my diminutive body to try to block all six feet plus of him from getting around me. He's stuck between me and the soundboard and lighting equipment; the only escape would be to walk out onstage.

He sighs heavily. "I don't want your gratitude, Alex. Don't you get that?" He puts his hand over the mic under his shirt.

"Well, I'm sorry, but I can't help it. You're saving my butt and I appreciate it." It's so weird to be whisper-yelling this at him, especially when the audio guy glances up and gives us both a dirty "shut up" look.

"So what happens now?" There's a tiny smile he tries to hide that confirms for me how ridiculous I must look using all 120 pounds of me and my 10-pound makeup bag to block him into this corner.

"We're talking about whatever it is we're not talking about." Clear as mud. He just looks at me. "You know what I mean."

"Can we do it after? I'm going on in a second." He

nods toward the stage manager, who I can now see in the dark waving his script, gesturing us forward.

"Yes. Of course," willing to be conciliatory, as long as he agrees to talk. I step aside pseudo-graciously and watch Billy talk briefly to the stage manager. I still feel disgruntled and now also embarrassed for almost interrupting production.

"I'll be right back," Billy whispers, coming back over to me. "Don't go anywhere." He says it in a joking tone, but his eyes aren't laughing. I nod back at him and turn to watch the monitor as he goes out onstage with a Texas swagger and a little extra twang in his voice. The consummate professional—you would never know from his quick interview and very funny sketch bit that he was under any kind of pressure at all.

"**WHAT WAS YOUR** boyfriend doing here?" The minute Billy's handed the mic back to the audio guy offstage, he catches me off guard with the direct question.

"What?" The out-of-left-field subject change is taking all the air out of me.

"I heard Nick Slants saying something to you about your boyfriend being downstairs when he got here. Is he here in New York?

"Um, yes, he kind of showed up here, I had no idea,"

I stammer, keeping pace with him as we head back to the dressing room area.

"Were you going to say anything to me about it?"

"I wasn't keeping it from you. We've had so much going on, and he just appeared out of nowhere."

"Right. Okay." He checks his watch. "I set the time for six so Nick would have a chance to pull his shit together. So let's talk about it now." Somehow his tone doesn't seem to fit the offer. But his voice is back to normal volume since we've exited the heavy soundstage doors.

"Sean showed up at the studio when we thought it was Nick waiting for me downstairs. It was Sean."

"Why? What'd he want?" We're in his assigned dressing room now. Billy kicks the door shut and peels the fancy dress shirt off over his head without even unbuttoning it.

"He asked me to come home." It's difficult carrying on a conversation with a half-dressed Billy Fox; as it turns out, the subject matter does not stop me from getting distracted by the view. *Focus, Alex*. I don't want him to think I was keeping secrets. "He proposed to me."

Billy turns to me, his worn Texas A&M sweatshirt in his hands. "What did you say?"

"Well, I never got the chance to say anything. That's when I saw Nick, so I just got rid of Sean as quickly as I could."

"Got rid of him how?" He pulls the maroon sweatshirt over his head and I'm distracted by wanting to run my fingers through his messy blond hair. He brushes a hand carelessly through it before bringing my focus back to the point. "What is Sean thinking right now?"

"About me and him? I have no idea." That's not quite true. "He thinks I'm thinking about it."

"Are you?" he asks, casually leaning against the small dressing table in the room. After I finished his makeup earlier, he'd switched off the neon overhead lights, so the room is now softly lit by the row of Hollywood makeup lights around the small mirror. It makes it hard to see his face in the shadows.

"No. I'm not. I don't want to go back," I say to him firmly. "I don't blame you if you don't believe me, after the way I've leaned on you to help me through this whole disaster. But that's not who I am anymore. I want to stand on my own two feet, clean up my own messes, and marry someone who wants me for me. Not the package that comes with my parents' construction company. I'm not a line item on an acquisitions spreadsheet."

"Who are you convincing? Me or yourself?" He's still backlit by the mirror and lights. And I have no idea what he's thinking from the tone of his voice.

"You. Me. I don't know, all of the above. It doesn't matter what I say, though, I have to actually do it." I only have one step to pace away from him. But I can't help it. I slam my bag on the ground and kick my foot against the wall. Frustration is practically choking me. "I keep saying I want to take care of myself, but every time there's a problem I would always run home to Dad. And then Sean. I thought a fresh start in New York would be enough to break the cycle, but apparently not. Here I am, in the middle of another disaster. Only difference is you're helping me instead of them."

"That's not quite how I see it." He hasn't moved a muscle, but there is so much warmth in his tone that I can feel his smile. "Are you kidding me? I had to force you to let me help you, Alex. That's not repeating bad behavior. Letting me be a part of your plan is just plain ol' common sense."

"No, I should have figured out a way without involving you . . . or anyone else, for that matter," I add, thinking of how Janeé and Andy and the others could get in trouble for helping me.

"There's a difference between getting other people to solve your problems for you and asking your friends for help when you need it. A big difference." Somehow the room seems so much smaller as Billy moves closer to me.

"Not really," I say. Trying to stay strong, I deny the easy out he's giving me.

"Alex, believe me. There are a lot of people out there who willingly play the victim at every opportunity. Maybe you were like that in the past, but you certainly aren't now. The woman I know is strong, tough, and willing to go for broke when she knows she's right." He smooths my hair behind my ear and then leans his hand against the wall by my head so he can lean in closer. "I'm not the one pulling the strings here. Sure, I asked a friend to help me prank a nasty reporter. You're the one risking everything, as much as I hate it. You had to get Slants to up the ante by going live. You're the one who will have to make this news tonight. And you're the one who will have to convince that editor and Hillary's lawyer that it's enough. You're doing those things, not me." It's hard not to believe him when his smoky voice is so passionately washing over me.

"Well, since you put it that way..." I let out a short laugh. His lips are so close to mine, I can feel his breath. I start to reach forward to close the gap when I feel a firm hand on my shoulder.

"Don't get me wrong, sweetheart. I want to kiss you right now more than anything." He's staring at my lips, but then he blinks. When he reopens his bright blue eyes, they're gazing intently into mine. "But I think you need to sort a few things out with that man who's waiting for an answer from you. Don't you?"

CHAPTER TWENTY

It's 7:52 a.m. and I'm standing outside a huge skyscraper on Sixth Avenue sipping the Starbucks latte I sprung for this morning. I need the caffeine dose to back up the extra cover-up I had to layer underneath my eyes to hide the dark circles. I've been standing here since seven o'clock waiting for Liz Daniels, attempting to appear much more confident than I feel.

As the managing editor of one of the most powerful magazines in the country finally gets out of her town car, I juggle the papers tucked under my arm. Mixed in with the tabloids hot off the presses are printouts I spent the early-morning hours compiling from every blog post and online article I could find detailing Nick Slants's fall from grace.

Apparently I've wasted several trees, because Ms. Daniels does not proceed to the revolving doors or in any way try to evade me. In fact, to my surprise, she meets my eyes and steps directly up to me.

"You've been busy," she says, assessing me.

"Nick Slants brought it on himself." I find myself feeling defensive.

"Of that I have no doubt." She looks at the fistful of papers I am still clutching with the tenacity of someone who knows her livelihood is on the line. "So? Tell me," she prompts.

"Nick Slants went live on his website last night with a story that was completely false. He had no real sources, and he'd done no real research, so he embarrassed himself by hyping up his big 'exclusive' exposing some Hollywood sex scandal, which turned out to be a couple actors rehearsing a scene for a movie. It seems clear if he's ever taken seriously as a journalist again, it won't be for a very long time."

"Nick has successfully walked that tightrope for years. How lucky for you that he crashed and burned when you needed him to most." I'm face-to-face with a woman who has successfully risen to the top of a dog-eat-dog industry, and she's not afraid to let me know it.

"Given his current reputation, your magazine won't publish his byline probably ever. And you're unlikely to get scooped by anyone else, am I right? No one will take him seriously, not for years."

Liz Daniels finally takes the papers from my hands. She leafs through several pages before handing them back to me, and finally I see a hint of personality slip through her ironclad shield. "Impressive." A tiny smile appears at the very edges of her perfectly lined lips. "No, I won't print anything Nick Slants brings me. No legitimate publication will."

"Can I get that in writing?"

I CHECK MY WATCH as Janeé waves me through building security with a knowing smirk. It's 9:51 a.m. and I wouldn't put it past Hillary P. and her lawyer to hold me to the ten o'clock deadline. Squeezing the pocket of my purse for the reassuring presence of my phone has become a nervous tic since I stole someone's cab at Sixth and Fifty-seventh. I was right to set aside my principles in healthy appreciation for morning rush hour Midtown traffic. Finally the elevator arrives and it's a fully loaded cab as we head back up to the thirty-seventh floor. Nine fifty-four. Which you'd think means I'll make it, except in New York, people ride the elevator for just one floor, so by the time we get to thirty-seven, we've stopped at almost every level in between. I'm starting to sweat as I sprint-walk down the hallways toward Hillary's private dressing room area.

I knock on her door without waiting to catch my breath, and so when Fircham opens it, one hand is still clutching the stitch in my side. Casually, I use the back of that hand to pat away the beads of sweat that are gathering on my upper lip. I've seen enough Discovery Channel to know I don't want either of these sharks to smell blood in the water.

"You're back," Hillary P. states, nonplussed.

"You made the deadline." Fircham looks at his Rolex, confirming it. "Just barely."

"We had an agreement," I say with all the confidence I can muster. After everything Billy did, the gauntlet we both survived over the last forty-eight hours, this is the real moment of truth. I have to convince them it's enough.

"Well?" Hillary deadpans. Immediately I'm thrown and pause for a second to regroup. Unlike Liz Daniels this morning, either Hillary has not been kept informed of the downfall of Nick Slants or she's playing dumb to make me work for it. I'd be a fool to assume the first.

"If you've been following the big Hollywood story since last night, you know that Nick Slants has publicly made a fool of himself. If anyone took him seriously as a reporter or a journalist before last night, they certainly don't now, and they very likely never will again."

"So? What does that have to do with what you did?" She's been doing her best *Goodfellas* impression, staring me down, but now she casually turns to lean into her beauty mirror to examine her lipstick. "You broke your deal, telling stories about me to the press. It doesn't matter that he's a fool. It doesn't change anything."

Up until now I was addressing Hillary. Confronting Hillary. It hadn't occurred to me that she wouldn't get it, but I know the lawyer will. Fircham has been silent behind me. No way am I going to let him off the hook.

"What Nick Slants did last night changes everything. He brought himself to national attention with a supposed jaw-dropping breaking story, and it turned out to be a big hoax. He had nothing, no sources, no journalistic integrity. He took one out-of-context quote and blew it up into this huge story that was nothing but hot air. Something I think we all already knew he was capable of." I include Hillary in that. I'm sure she'd love the opportunity to save her pride by believing Nick's story about her was equally unfounded.

Fircham walks over to his briefcase and some files he has stacked on Hillary's dainty coffee table. I wait for him to say something, to tear up the confidentiality agreement. I wanted some grand gesture to let me know it's finally over. But he doesn't do anything. He just looks up at me, above the rim of his reading glasses, and says, "Go on."

"Don't you see?" I look between both of them. "With the beating Nick Slants's reputation is taking all over the media, he's a laughingstock. His story is sparking a debate this morning all over the news about the journalistic integrity issues with bloggers and social media. No one will take him seriously. Meaning that he won't be able to publish that article about Hillary at all. No one will pay him a penny for his story."

"He could still post it online. It still exists," Hillary interjects.

"True," I have to concede, but Fircham's unblinking stare warns me not to get distracted. "But there's no power behind it now. Anything he posts will be ignored or mocked. So it's better than shutting down this one article, or my quotes. You have the confidence of knowing that no matter what Nick Slants says, no one will listen."

Fircham keeps his eyes on me as he rises and walks the few steps to where Hillary is simmering in the corner. They confer quietly. The lawyer's voice is rational and low while Hillary's whispering borders on hysterical.

"I'm just supposed to take her word for it?!" Her shrill screech is impossible not to hear.

"No, you don't have to take my word for it." Both heads turn back to me. I reach into my purse and grab my iPhone, which hasn't been out of my grasp since I left Liz Daniels. Quickly flicking through the menu, I press play on the video I swore to delete the second this meeting is over.

"Hillary, it's been a long time." I hold out the phone so both Hillary and Fircham can see and hear it clearly. Hillary leans in to stare closely at the video image of Liz Daniels on my screen. "We've had our differences over the years, but you and I both know that image is everything. Today, one nasty piece of trash is getting what it deserves." She pauses, and I swear I can see Hillary's complexion pale under her too heavily applied foundation. "But it's not you. I won't publish Nick Slants's exposé, and neither will anyone else. Your secret is safe." And then silence.

Hillary is still for a moment before making a sudden grab at my phone. I wasn't expecting it, but I've been so tense I manage to hold on to the phone in spite of her lunge. Instinctively jumping back a step, Fircham reaches up to physically restrain his client. "Just take it from her. That nasty bitch. Who does she think she is?" Hillary unleashes a torrent of filth at me, Liz Daniels, and even her lawyer as he unsuccessfully tries to calm her down. Hillary slaps his hands away, curses at him again, and slams into her private bathroom, where we hear several things shatter.

Completely unfazed by Hillary's tantrum, Fircham reaches out to shake my hand. "Ms. Cleary, I'm glad we could come to an understanding. You've proven your point, and I think we can all put this little matter behind us." I shake it, my eyes darting to the door as the cursing and crashing continue unabated.

"One more thing before I go, Mr. Fircham. I had this drawn up." His brows immediately furrow as I reach into my purse for the letter. "It states that I understand I am still bound by the nondisclosure I signed, and will continue to act accordingly. As Hillary"—I hesitate—"or her representative, agrees that this one incident regarding private nonspecific statements I made unknowingly to Mr. Slants is not to be held against me now or in the future."

It's grown suspiciously quiet as Hillary's lawyer reviews the simple paragraph. Billy's lawyer helped me draft it, but I wanted it to be as straightforward as possible. No room for loopholes.

"Yes, this looks in order." He side-eyes me. "Good work."

"Thank you," I reply as he pulls a fountain pen from his inner coat pocket and signs with a flourish. He hands me the pen and I sign as well.

"I'd like to keep this, if you don't mind," he says coolly, reaching for the paper.

"Wait." Wishing I'd thought to make copies, I pull out my phone again and just as I snap a close-up picture of the letter, the bathroom door slams open.

Hillary sweeps back into the room, her attention directed only at her lawyer. "Please get her out of my private space, Douglas." She leans heavily on the back of a chair. "I just can't bear the sight of her. I want this whole mess over, now."

"Yes, of course, Hillary. She's leaving *now*." Giving nothing away with his facial expression, Fircham calmly opens the door, blocking her view of me as I walk out. It takes a few steps for me to wrap my head around what just happened. Really, it's not until I'm at the elevator banks waiting to head downstairs that I feel my cheeks almost aching from my ear-to-ear grin.

TWENTY MINUTES LATER, I still haven't found a cab, and I don't even care. The pedestrians walking past me keep shooting me dirty "she must not be from here" looks. The visual of how my hand waving ineffectually in the air and my dopey smile must look to strangers makes me giggle. Finally a taxi pulls over and, still floating on cloud nine, I hop in, ignoring my usual germ issues.

After giving the cabbie the address, I sit back, reliving the conversation with Hillary so that I can recount everything for Billy as accurately as possible. Thinking of the look on his face when I show him the video I took of Liz Daniels, I am caught totally off guard when his voice suddenly fills the cab. After a second of disorientation, I realize it's coming from the TV screen in the center console. Wow, they already have Billy's *Late Night* interview up? But then no…it's not Billy they're talking about. It's an entertainment news story about Nick's live disaster.

"Last night, in what is being described online as an epic journalistic fail, Nick Slants publicly revealed himself and his incompetence all at once." There's a cut to the shaky low-resolution footage of Nick standing out front of the artists' entrance to my old West Side studio.

"I'm here at the hidden back-alley entrance to one of the legendary studios in New York City. You may not recognize me, but I'm Nick Slants. A reporter willing to stop at nothing to get to the truth."

"Ha. He wouldn't recognize truth if it hit him in the face," I say at the cab TV screen.

"But as it turns out, Mr. Slants has a very different definition of 'truth,'" the newscaster says before the camera cuts back to Nick.

"I have been following the sex scandal of the century. When I discovered the level of atrocities being committed by these so-called celebrities, I knew I had only one choice: to come forward and speak for the innocent and abused victims. There are probably going to be some depraved and immoral acts going on behind these closed doors. I am broadcasting this to you live to make sure the criminals are forced to take responsibility. But what you are about to see is not for the faint of heart." I roll my eyes, and then he is kicking in the door, quickly followed by his cameraman.

Me: Good thing you decided to leave that door unlocked.
Billy: yeah, it's great the way the door just slams open and there we all are, with scripts and water bottles. Bailey thought of laying down rehearsal "marks" on the ground right before he got there.

I look up from reading Billy's text to see what he's talking about. There are little white T's made of gaffers tape all over the floor. The situation is clearly a bunch of actors caught in the middle of rehearsals. It's impossible not to laugh out loud at the look of sincere shock they all manage to fake.

Me: That is genius. Remind me to thank Bailey. You all deserve Oscars for your performances. Jared was hilarious with his mad improv skillz.

"But the never-say-die Nick Slants didn't just give up there, no." Back to the newscaster, clearly relishing this story. "He tries to interrogate Billy Fox, of all people. One of Hollywood's, if not America's, all-around good guys. Get a load of this."

The edit is back to Nick shoving the handheld mic in Billy's face. "Wait, who the hell are you? And what are you even accusing me of?" The replay shows Billy giving a suitably confused and appalled expression to the camera.

"I am Nick Slants, and I'm here exposing you as part of this illicit sex ring. I overheard you, Billy, at the Lion's Den last night." Nick is coming on strong, like the detectives on *NCIS*. Sitting in the cab now, I marvel at how willing Nick was to believe such a ridiculous story.

"Wow...so you're Nick Slants." Billy begins to crack up laughing. "Hey, you guys—this is that sleazy reporter, that Slants guy. Wait'll you hear what he's come up with this time." His voice is shaking with laughter, and the actors behind him snicker but don't seem alarmed. You can hear Nick's camera guy trying to contain a chuckle as the camera shakes for a second. One dirty look from Nick, though, and the camera settles. I can practically see the steam coming from Nick's ears. I smile in the cab. Even a hundred viewings later, this hasn't gotten old.

"There is nothing about this to laugh about," Nick sputters, getting all morally superior. "How dare you make light of this heinous crime? You and your celebrity friends, hiring minors? Forcing drugs on them?"

Billy sobers up quickly. "I'm laughing at you, Slants. Not the subject matter."

"So, you're willing to protect your friends from this sex scandal, but not protect innocent teenagers from your disgusting habits?!"

"Nick, you've lost your mind." Billy shakes his head, looks around. "Hey, y'all. Nick Slants thinks we're running some sort of illegal sex ring." His drawl serves to emphasize the ridiculousness of the accusation. The camera pans around the empty room as the five actors gather gym bags. I see Bailey highlighting something on a script. They all react nonplussed at Billy's announcement.

"I heard you planning it at the Lion's Den." Nick just won't give up the ghost. "A club notorious for its tolerance of illegal activity," he adds to the pixelated camera streaming the whole incident live to Nick's own website.

"I know what you heard, Nick." Billy turns back to the camera, finally seeming irritated. "While I'm not shocked that you were obviously listening in on my conversation in the men's room, it's a bit surprising how bad you are at getting accurate information." I believe in chess that would be a check for Billy. The clip continues as Billy addresses the camera, as if Nick does not deserve this explanation. "I'm developing a new movie for next year. A really dark look at the prostitution and human slavery rings that are really going on around the world. It's a terrifying global problem and I wanted to shed light on it. The studio and I have been pitching this idea around for a while now, and we finally got the full concept together. Nick seems to have overheard some key words and started leaping to pretty ridiculous conclusions." The camera cuts to Nick, his mouth agape. "Perhaps you should try gathering real evidence before you start slandering people, Nick. Now, I'm no lawyer, but that is the only real crime here." Checkmate.

The news story ends with a bit of advice from a gleeful newscaster thrilled at bringing down this former rival. "Nick, as a professional reporter, all I can say is you need to learn a thing or two about journalism. It's more than just a one-hundred-twenty-character tweet." The news segment ends on a freeze frame of Billy's charming smile.

CHAPTER TWENTY-ONE

It's impossible to describe how light I feel tonight. I look around at the smiling faces of Billy's friends; we pulled this impromptu dinner together for a Sunday night victory celebration. Everyone is laughing, toasting one another, or recounting their part in our masquerade. Emma showed up. She brought Andy and a few discreet members of the Hillary P. crew whom I'd bonded with in my brief time there. It's only been a couple of days, but as Andy recounts for me Monica's abuse of the new makeup artist, it all seems so far away now.

"I'm glad you're free, Alex." Andy raises his beer mug to clink with my wineglass. "What are you going to do now? Go back to California?"

"I hope not." Billy leans back to interject in our conversation. Glancing over my shoulder at him, I look back to catch some mysterious masculine look exchanged between them. I'd thought Billy was engrossed in his conversation with Sophie and her husband. How did he even know what we were talking about?

"Never mind him," I say to Andy, reminding myself that I'm seeing Sean first thing tomorrow morning. Then I can move on once and for all. "I'm not sure what I'm going to do now. Certainly, I think it would be best to keep off Hillary's radar. But I think I'd like to stay in New York if I can build up some clients here." Already Selma has asked if I can do her makeup for an event tomorrow night, so I'm feeling like I might just be able to make it work here in Manhattan. But there's a lot left to sort out, like a place to live.

"I'm sorry I couldn't help more." Emma finally approaches me privately as I'm opening more wine bottles in Billy's pristine kitchen. She's been relatively reserved, and I'm surprised she even came.

"I probably would have done the same thing," I say quickly. As the words are still coming out of my mouth, they feel wrong. I don't know for sure, but I'd like to think I wouldn't turn my back on a friend in trouble. "You did what you had to do." Which sounds closer to the truth. I'm not going to throw my drink in her face and make a *Real Housewives*–style scene over it. She was looking out for herself, and I understand that.

"No. I was selfish. I was protecting my own ass. When you needed me most." I'm surprised to see her usually calm face actually tighten up briefly. I'd like to blame the alcohol, but the moisture I see filling her eyes makes mine start to burn, too. "I will never forgive myself for not being there for you..."

"Stop it, Emma," I interrupt, and hug her quickly. "We're fine. Really." I look her in the eye, and she meets my gaze briefly before her eyes fall away. And after a few more casual words, I let her drift back into the crowd.

I'M STILL THINKING about Emma later, helping Billy clean up from the spontaneous party.

"It'll be all right, you know. You two will get past it," Billy says, heading to the kitchen with another load of wineglasses.

"I said everything was fine. But it isn't. It was so awkward. Like she was waiting for me to bitch her out. And when I said it was okay, that I understand, she wasn't like, 'Oh, that's amazing, you're the best friend ever'... God, it was like she was disappointed."

"Well, maybe she was." Billy's voice echoes through the now empty apartment. I follow the sound to find him putting away the cigar box he'd brought out earlier. His study is completely different from the rest of his place. Dark, overstuffed leather chairs are arranged on stained woodwork, and as I look up I see the cutout in the ceiling indicating a drop-down projector screen. "Want to watch a movie?" he asks when he sees what I'm looking at.

"Ha, no. It's pretty late. I just haven't been back here. It's different. Nice." I sometimes still find myself awkwardly stammering in front of Billy. Even after everything we've been through, or maybe because of all that…it's hard to feel comfortable with things so unresolved. Sometimes I feel like his girlfriend; clearly I'm someone he's willing to stick his neck out for. And sometimes I feel like what I really am—a girl he's been out with twice, whose life is a complete train wreck.

"Okay," he says easily, but his attention is on reorganizing his humidor. I like seeing him be a bit compulsive, just like me making sure every makeup brush is cleaned and put back exactly where it belongs.

"What did you mean about Emma?" I ask, remembering what had brought me back here in the first place. "About her being disappointed?"

Billy doesn't answer right away. He puts the box back on the shelf and comes to stand in front of me. "You let her off the hook pretty easily. Maybe she needed you to rake her over the coals a bit. She certainly deserved it." He shrugs, just stating facts.

"She's my friend. It's over. I just want to forget about it."

"I get that, Alex. But that's not really gonna happen, now is it?" His Texas twang is a little more noticeable after a few cocktails and his voice is even smokier from the cigars. "It's gonna just sit and fester. What you gotta do is get it all off your chest. And she needs to hear it."

He lays his warm palm against my cheek and looks me in the eyes for a minute.

"Clearly confrontations are not my thing," I admit frankly. Though he probably already figured that out on his own. "I'm meeting Sean at the High Line tomorrow at ten. Maybe I can see Emma after she gets off work."

"Sounds like a plan." He rubs his thumb across my lower lip, but then pulls away. "Good night, Alex." Off he goes, toward the master bedroom at the far end of the apartment. And I head to my guest room in the opposite direction.

CHAPTER TWENTY-TWO

❧

"I brought you a cappuccino. One sugar." Sean hands me the warm to-go cup with a satisfied smile on his face. I can tell that in his mind, he just chalked up another point for himself. I used to keep score too, reflecting back. But it's time to let all that go.

"How 'bout we walk a bit?" I'm starting to sound like Billy. Grinning inwardly, I gesture toward the High Line park stretching out in front of us, above the busy city streets. It's an amazing bit of greenery growing up out of unused elevated train tracks. We walk for a bit down the path, passing New Yorkers lying out on lounge chairs. I still haven't adapted to the weather. It's sunny today, but still quite chilly, and yet the true locals take any opportunity to shed their winter gear. You can tell the true New York natives by the way they're wearing T-shirts and even tank tops, just grateful for any vitamin D. I shiver in my lined trench coat just imagining it.

"It's so cold here, how do you stand it?" Sean asks, clearly noticing the same thing.

"You get used to it." I'm affirming it for myself as much as for him.

"Well, good thing you'll be back in sunny SoCal soon enough. I bet you'll be glad to ditch the long johns, right?" I walk another couple of steps without answering.

"It's been almost a week...have you thought about what I said?" he finally asks. There's definitely a change in Sean too, I notice. He would never have been so patient before.

"Yes, of course I have." I lie awake all night figuring out the right words. And now my pretty speech seems trite and unimportant. "Sean, so much has changed since I left."

"It's only been a couple months, Alex. Come on, now." See, that's more like the Sean I know.

"I'm not going back to LA." Saying it out loud for the first time, all of a sudden it seems more right than ever. "I like me here in New York. Even when it's cold. Even when I'm scared out of my mind that I'm going to crash and burn. I know I'm in charge of my own life. And I've never felt so alive."

"What are you talking about, Alex? You sound like a Tony Robbins billboard." He steps in my path to stop me. "Have you met someone else? Is that it? That guy I saw you talking to after you said you had to go back to work?"

He saw me with Nick? "No. Not him. Definitely not him. That was work," I add, shrugging at the irony that it was, in fact, work related.

"Oh, then someone else? How many? Have you been just playing the field here, is that it? That's fine. You were mad at me, and rebelling against your parents, I get it." He has it all figured out.

"Give it a break, Sean." Only slightly offended by his characterization of me, I continue. "This isn't about that. And you know it. The bottom line is, you don't really want me. You want the whole package. My family, their business...I know that. I've always known that. And it used to be good enough. And now it's not."

His silence is confirmation I didn't really need.

"My parents love you. They trust you. You have nothing to worry about."

"I don't know why you're saying all that." Sean seems to have regrouped. "This has nothing to do with them, and I can't believe you think that." It takes me a second to realize he's not just fighting the good fight. He chucks his half-full coffee cup into a nearby trash can and comes back to get right in my face. "I'm not the right guy now, and that's fine. I can live with that. Maybe I'm not good enough for you." He takes a deep breath, his eyes never leaving mine. "But I never used you, Alex."

And without another word he turns around and disappears down the High Line. I watch him go, sort of stunned by how badly that all turned out, but his dark nylon jacket fades quickly into the crowded walkway. I take a seat recently vacated by a college student hurrying off and sip my coffee.

As I watch colorful tourists, locals, families, and vagrants all pass by, I realize I have a perfect snapshot of Manhattan right here in front of me. The good, the bad, and the crazy. I just know I want to be here in it. And maybe Billy is a part of that decision. Okay, a big part. But it's also for me. This city has brought out the best in me, and I'm going to fight to hold on to this part of me with all I've got.

"LOOK DOWN, but don't close all the way." I gesture with my hand to a point low enough that I can use Bailey's natural eye shape to apply the smoky eye shadow correctly.

"So are you and Billy exclusive?" the actress asks while adjusting her smartphone to the exact position that allows her to keep her eyes lowered as I requested but still text at the same time.

"We haven't really talked about it."

"Why not?"

"Look at me." Using the job to distract her, I judge

both eyelids to make sure they are even. "Okay, down again." I pull out a Q-tip to blend in the left side a bit more.

"You know every woman in America is going to hate you when they see you with him," she says with more than a bit of relish.

"I hadn't even thought of that," I say with a laugh. And it's true. With all the things that stress me out about dating Billy, what other women will think, or even being in the spotlight, isn't one of them.

"Okay, then what's the holdup?" She meets my eyes in the mirror and tucks her phone under her slim torn-denim-clad thigh.

"There's no holdup," I say as I search through my little nylon bag of eye pencils for the exact shade of blue-black to enhance her eyes. When I find it, I look up again to find her still locked in on me. "What? Bailey, we're interested in each other; at this point, that's all." He may have walked away last night, but he won't tonight. I get shivers all over just thinking about it.

"Well, I think you should commit to this. To him. Like you did to staying here in New York. Why not?"

"For one thing, I'm not even sure Billy wants a commitment."

"Are you kidding me? If he wasn't serious about you he wouldn't have called out everyone but the National Guard to help you deal with Hillary P. And he definitely wouldn't have waited to sleep with you until you were for sure split up with your ex."

The intimacy of doing makeup gets me again... Usually it's the client divulging their secrets to the makeup artist. But it works both ways. And somewhere between blending in a sheer foundation and applying gorgeous over-the-top eyelash strips to draw focus to her big Disney eyes, Bailey and I connected. Having identified common ground—Billy was the starting point—I confided in her everything that happened last night.

"Maybe he just didn't want things to be messy."

"I've known him a long time. Billy doesn't spend a lot of time worrying about the backstory of the women he dates. You're different. He's different with you."

"Well, I'm happy about that. We'll take it slow. See how it goes." She gives an unladylike grunt. "Look left." I gently draw the dark pencil to the inner corner of her eye before repeating the process on the other side.

"Okay, that sounds fine, if mildly boring. Which is pretty much the last thing I expected to get from Billy Fox's love life."

"He's not boring." I rush to defend him.

"Is it you, then? Something else going on?"

"Oh, come on, Bailey." I get a smudge brush to go over the pencil line. "My life is essentially a do-over at this point. I have nowhere to live in a new, very expensive city, and I'm starting from scratch with my career.

I'm trying to be smart about this. If the situation was reversed, all my friends would be screaming at me to steer clear of a guy obviously looking for a meal ticket in the Big Apple."

"Nobody sees you that way." Bailey seems truly shocked by my representation of my situation.

"Well, you should. You should be looking out for your friend," I only half kiddingly reprimand her.

"I am," she says with authority. And for all her youth, there is no question she means what she says. "But if it bothers you so much, then do something about it."

"I'm working on it," I mutter, and decide it's time to apply Bailey's delicate rose lip liner, which has the helpful side effect of ending the conversation.

BY THE TIME dinner arrives, I'm a bundle of nerves. We've been seated in a booth in this very chic restaurant on the Lower East Side. The hostess recognized Billy instantly and brought us to a table in the back with a view of the entire restaurant.

We laughed and talked casually as we looked through the menu, but now that the waiter has come and gone and our drinks are safely in our hands, I know it's time to get things on the table.

"So, I've come up with a plan," I begin.

"Okay..."

"I'm going to stay in New York." He just looks at me with an "of course you are" expression. "But I'm not going to be mooching off you, Billy. I want to figure stuff out for myself, be independent." I keep going when he looks like he's going to argue. "I want to work hard and earn my place in this city. Do you understand?"

Billy sighs and grabs one of my hands, which is clutching my cocktail glass, to pull it to his lips for a kiss. "Yes, crazy girl. I understand. And I respect your determination. I would love to help you, any way I can."

And later that night, as we're lying exhausted and naked in his bed, he props himself up on one elbow to look down at me, snuggling next to him, still catching my breath. I pry open one eye to see him smiling, and I almost want to cry from the feelings in his expression. "I believe in you," he whispers. And when he kisses me softly, I feel a tear sneaking out.

CHAPTER TWENTY-THREE

~

Billy's lovely sentiment and the memory of his dreamy kisses keep me warm the next day as New York shows off her bipolar nature with a very cold breeze whipping down the avenues. I've dropped off my résumé at MAC, Stila, and Henri Bendel. I decide to make a personal call to a studio I visited with Hillary last month for a photo shoot.

"Hey, Joe, I was just in the neighborhood and I wanted to let you know I'm available to do beauty makeup if you ever have photo shoots and need someone." I pause, imagining hearing the obvious reply in my head. "What happened with Hillary?" I ask myself the hard-hitting questions, practicing an answer for what will inevitably be on everyone's mind. "Oh, you know...I just want to test myself creatively. I loved working there, but I'm not into a routine." I try sounding carefree while still seeming like a reliable contact. Luckily not one of the hundreds of people I pass on Madison Avenue seems to notice me talking to myself.

Which I'm still doing when my phone rings. The screen reads UNKNOWN.

"Hello?"

"Ms. Cleary?"

"Yes, that's me," I reply, bracing myself for the hazards of answering a blocked number.

"This is Nicolette from Liz Daniels's office. I'm calling to see if you'd be available to come by right away to do some touch-ups on Ms. Daniels."

"Um…" The managing editor of *Identity* magazine wants me to do her makeup, and I don't even have my personal makeup stash with me in my purse today. "What time would you need me there?" After literally pounding the pavement all day, I have two blisters on each foot, and no job to speak of. I need to say yes to this opportunity if at all possible.

"Can you be here by four p.m.? She has to leave the office by five." That gives me forty minutes to get all the way uptown to grab my makeup kit from Billy's and then back to Midtown. I'll never make it.

"Does she need her hair done as well?" I stall while hailing a cab.

"No, she happened to visit her hairdresser during lunch. This is a last-minute event and our usual people are not available."

I mute the phone while she's talking, to direct the cabbie who has no idea he's just saved my day: "Eighty-third and Central Park West. Please, as quick as you can." Unmute. "I can be there by four-fifteen and it absolutely won't take me forty-five minutes to do her makeup." It occurs to me to double-check. "Just a beauty look, right? Not a special effect of any kind?"

"Yes, just beauty," she replies, and the relief in her voice is apparent. After we hang up, I wonder about why it would take an hour to do her makeup. Having met Ms. Daniels, I can't imagine she has the patience or flexibility to sit around getting her makeup done for sixty minutes.

I'm too rushed to really even celebrate this opportunity. I am staring at the minute hands on my watch as the cab jets us uptown. The driver is taking my clear impatience as license to weave in and out of traffic in a way I've only ever seen in police chases on the Channel 9 news in LA. But far from being scared, I am cheering him on every block.

"Please wait, I just have to grab my bag. I'll be right back," I say as I leap out of the cab in front of Billy's building. I wave at the doorman as I dash past, grateful he recognizes my blur and lets me in without hesitation. Billy isn't there when I use the key he gave me. I grab my bag from the hall closet and I'm back to the Mario Andretti of cabdrivers in less than five minutes.

"To Sixth?" he asks, clarifying the second destination we discussed.

"Yes. Thank you." It's 3:58. Twenty minutes to get

back to Midtown is cutting it close at this hour, but doable. I breathe and grab my phone to update Billy.

> **Me:** I'm doing Liz Daniels's makeup for some event tonight! I just got the offer.
> **Billy:** that's great. go get 'em.
> **Me:** Super psyched.

And then I remember I was supposed to meet Emma. New text.

> **Me:** I'm so sorry I can't make it to coffee. Just got a job, think this one could lead to more—hope you understand.
> **Emma:** Of course. Good luck. Really hope we can talk soon.

Her text is sweet, but it's easy to tell she's still feeling awkward after our last conversation.

> **Me:** I can meet up with you afterward? Drinks?
> **Emma:** Sounds like a plan.

The cab slams on the brakes in front of the massive building.

> **Me:** I'll text you later.

I throw money at the cabbie, making sure to tip him well for keeping us both in one piece. My phone says 4:10, which gets me up to her office right on time. Just the impression I need to make.

"I'M HERE TO see Ms. Daniels." I gesture to my makeup kit, and both her assistant and I smirk, appreciating the irony.

"Can I get you coffee or tea?" he asks, way more welcoming than the last time I stood in front of his desk.

"No thanks, I should probably set up. Where's a good place?"

"Oh, go on in. You have to just do what you can while she's working. She doesn't have time to leave her desk." It takes a second to process what he's said. I'm meant to apply makeup hunched over her office desk? While she's still making calls and typing on her computer? That seems impossible. No wonder past makeup artists insisted on an hour. It would take at least that long with a moving target.

I head into her fabulously appointed corner office. The huge picture windows allow plenty of light in; that's a plus. And pretty much the only one. Liz doesn't say much. I ask her what her dress looks like and she lifts one hand from her keyboard to point out a gorgeous bold floral-print gown hanging from a sconce on the far wall. There are strong reds and yellows in the print, and I can see the stylist has carried that bold theme into the red Manolos and yellow diamond chandelier earrings.

For the next fifty minutes it's like some sort of twisted video game. The foundation is pretty easy; she's got an earpiece in, and for the most part, she lets me adjust the angle of her face as I need to while she listens and engages in what seems like several different conversations at once. I lose a lot of time getting her eyes done. I have to keep walking around her chair to the other side to get access to her left eye, and while she shifts to allow me room at her computer, it's all just awkward and time-consuming.

I've just curled her eyelashes and am getting out brand-new mascara from my case when Nicolette, Liz's other assistant, walks in.

"The car is here, Ms. Daniels."

"Thank you, Nicolette." She pulls away from the desk and starts to gather her things. "Thank you for coming, Alex. Nicolette will take down your information and let you know where to send the invoice."

"But...I'm not done yet," I say, dumbfounded.

"Sorry, but she has to get dressed now." Nicolette comes next to me, ushering me out before I have a chance to think. "You can wait outside and collect your things when Ms. Daniels is gone."

Standing outside her office for a minute cools my head. When the door opens and Liz steps out looking like the fashion icon she is, I have a plan.

"Ms. Daniels, I'm going to come with you in the car so I can finish your makeup." I don't wait for a reply. If I've learned one thing working for powerful women, it's that I have to be strong, too. I grab a few essentials from the corner of her desk where I laid out my supplies while Liz is still switching a few things from her Hermes bag to a gorgeous small red satin clutch.

"That isn't appropriate," Nicolette stammers...

"Nonsense, Nicolette." Liz waves her off. "You won't have much time, though, Alex. The event is at the Natural History Museum."

"That's fine." I look at all my stuff strewn around her office. It looks like a tornado hit. "Can I come back here to pack up after you get dropped off?"

"Of course." She sails out of the office with me chasing after her, only thinking to stuff my cell phone in my back pocket, just in case.

IF I GET another chance to do Liz Daniels's makeup, I think I'll just wait in the car. She's trapped in one position, and even with her smartphone keeping her busy, I am quickly able to apply mascara and add false individual lashes to the outer edges of each eye. She doesn't seem like the type who will keep reapplying lip gloss throughout the evening, so I choose a deep pencil and matte lip stain. It goes on smoothly, since I've now figured out a strategy.

I wait for when she's listening intently to the person she's talking to and apply as quickly and efficiently as I can.

I slip the pencil into her clutch and gesture clearly to her that her purse is sitting next to her on the car seat. She nods distractedly. Finally finished, and satisfied with my work, I shift to the interior of the limo to pack up. I figure it will be better if the cameras don't see someone else sitting inside the limo when she gets out.

Since Liz is still deep in conversation, I just finish packing up and start checking my phone as we pull up.

"Thanks again, Alex." Liz draws my attention as she slips her phone into her purse as the door opens.

"No problem. I hope you're happy."

Finally realizing she hasn't even looked at my work, she flips down the mirror from the limo roof. She moves her head a bit to see both eyes and the shade of lip I chose. Since she offered no input along the way, I went with my gut. I hold my breath, waiting for her verdict. "I love it. Gorgeous, Alex. Really." And then the door is opened and our conversation is over. A gentleman in tails helps Liz out and her fabulous gown is engulfed by the waiting crowd of publicists and event organizers.

The limo has only just pulled away from the red carpet when I notice Liz's evening bag still lying on the backseat. I don't know Liz Daniels well, but I have no doubt she will flip out when she realizes she doesn't have her phone or anything with her.

"Sir?" I knock on the glass partition separating the back from the driver's section. When it starts to lower, I say, "Ms. Daniels left her purse. We need to go back."

"Yes, ma'am." But in the crush of Manhattan traffic, in a stretch limo, it isn't an easy feat. We circle the block, coming back around to the red carpet.

The driver assures me he'll stay there while I go in. The front of the museum is swarmed with people, and the lights flashing as paparazzi photograph celebrities on the red carpet are blinding to everyone. There is pop music keeping the energy up and an announcer introducing people getting out of limos to the crowd of fans behind the barricades.

I catch the attention of someone with credentials around his neck. "Excuse me, Liz Daniels left her purse in the car. I need to get this to her."

"Sorry, I can't let you on the carpet." I instantly decide not to trust this harried-looking kid with Liz Daniels's cell phone. "You'll have to go that way." And he fades into the crowd after vaguely pointing toward the other side of the carpet, where the photographers and press are all busy talking to and taking pictures of the glamorous.

Following his suggestion, I slip behind the photographers and easily move along the working underbelly of the red carpet. It's definitely a strange point of view. But I quickly spot Liz Daniels being interviewed up ahead, so I shuffle toward her.

It's only when I get closer to Liz that I see Hillary P. is in the press line as well. A quite desperate-looking publicist is holding her back. I quickly turn away, hoping she didn't see me, and keep inching my way closer through producers and sound engineers, trying to get to Liz's position. I am grateful for the crews behind all the cameras blocking my progress from Hillary's view, but I see her subtly jerk her arm away from the petite, agitated blonde, and she disappears from view.

Getting into Liz's eye line, I hold up her purse to answer the confused look on her face. She interrupts her interview to gesture me forward. The *Entertainment Tonight* crew makes room for me to come to the edge of the red carpet.

"Oh, Alex. You are a lifesaver. Thank you!" Liz Daniels air-kisses both my cheeks. I respond appropriately, but am immediately distracted by the chance to reassess her hair and makeup under the lights.

"One second," I say over my shoulder to the handsome reporter getting his mic ready to restart the interview. I pull the sponge out of the compact I'd stuffed in her purse and run it quickly under her eyes. After removing the smudge that had appeared in the few moments since she'd left me, I smoothly powder the center of her forehead and run my fingers through her hair, shaking out the curls to add some body to the short style. "Okay, you're good."

"My new makeup artist; she's meticulous. I love it." Liz laughs and reengages with the camera. Liz's approval has me on cloud nine as I fade back behind the cameras and lights. With no urgency now, I decide to go with the flow to the end of the carpet rather than trying to go upstream. As I get to where the online celebrity news bloggers and podcasters are fighting to get time with their favorites, there's an empty spot being trampled by the others that has NICK SLANTS written in bold computer font. I quickly look around, but he is nowhere to be seen. Not feeling sorry at all, I finally break free of the craziness and look for an exit.

A woman standing on the #HOMECOOKSUNITE sign grabs the arm of the webcam operator in front of me, and they take off. I'm starting to follow, hoping they're headed toward an exit too, when I hear a familiar grating voice. I can tell instantly that Hillary's close to the edge.

"Get the camera ready," the slightly plump home cook whispers to her friend. "I'll just ask for a picture, but be ready to go to video in case she gives me advice or says something amazing."

I'm right behind them, but while I spend a second thinking of how to suggest that maybe this isn't a good idea, her friend replies, "I'll just record the whole thing. We can pull a still from it for your photo album."

"Perfect." And they round the corner as Hillary's voice hits a pitch I know is bad news. Pressed up against a huge flag promoting the evening's powerhouse performances, I am crushed up between a larger-than-life Justin Timberlake poster and the wall. I hold as still as possible, not wanting to be seen by Hillary. But then I can't help but turn my head to watch through the blogger's screen as she videos the fan approaching Hillary P.

She zooms in a bit, watching the screen instead of the live action. I think we both feel a bit removed from what's happening. Hillary shoves her purse and coat at a young man next to her. There's no mistaking her physicality; he stumbles a bit from the force of it hitting his chest. I remember him from set. Kevin had been just starting out as an intern to the producing team. Clearly he's moved up in rank to Hillary's latest victim.

"Don't you ever interrupt me again," she spits out, not paying attention to the fan whose excited smile quickly fades away as Hillary gets in Kevin's face. She lashes out a string of curses belittling and humiliating him, clearly oblivious to her audience.

"Hillary, please wait. I was just trying to fix something on your dress. The hanger strap was showing. I knew you'd be upset when you saw it in pictures." Poor kid. Damned either way.

"Well, you should've seen it before you embarrassed me in front of the reporters. And then you allowed Liz Daniels to get in front of me in the press line? Do you know how humiliating that is?"

Before she's finished, my eyes focus on the little red dot blinking steadily on the camera's viewfinder. The cheerful fan is now beet red but seems frozen in place. Hillary doesn't let up on her prey. "I will destroy your entire life. You think you can fuck with me? Now go get me that interview with CNN or consider yourself fired." She spins away from him only to stop, face-to-face with the two women who'd so enthusiastically sought out a fan picture.

On the camera screen, I can see her charming mask easily slide back into place. But the devastated face of Kevin as he darts off and the silent reproachful woman who saw it all unnerve Hillary.

"You were eavesdropping on a private conversation." Without missing a beat, Hillary jumps into the no-defense-like-a-good-offense strategy.

"I was just hoping for a picture," the woman says simply. "I got a pretty clear one." And then both former fans turn and disappear back into the red carpet chaos. I stand still not a foot away from Hillary, hidden from her view by the Justin Timberlake poster. I have to hold my breath to prevent it from swaying. I can't see her expression without the fan's camera there, but I don't need to. I realize all of a sudden the cramped quarters I am stuck in until Hillary leaves. I brace myself for the panic to start suffocating me. But it doesn't. I will my shoulders to relax, and then the knots in my stomach. And they do. I am able to wait patiently until I'm sure she's gone before coming around to see what's happening: There is an entire cocktail party in full force on the steps up to the grand entrance.

I weave my way back through the crews of reporters who are interviewing big-name celebrities still filing down the red carpet. Back on the street packed with stretch limos and black Mercedes sedans, I take a deep breath only to realize I don't really need one. The lights have the trees of Central Park lit up as the setting sun adds shades of pink and purple to the sky above the tall buildings.

Liz Daniels's driver isn't anywhere to be found. It's impossible to figure out which car is which as I wind my way toward the maze of black sedans and limos. And then a familiar dark blond head steps out of a black Mercedes sedan right in front. Billy would stand out in any situation, but his casual Henley tee and dark jeans enhance the effect. It takes only a few steps for me to reach his side.

"What are you doing here?" I ask.

His smile melts my insides. "That fan video of Hillary is going viral."

"Really? That seems pretty quick..." I stop as Billy just smirks at me. "Did you link to it?" Billy's millions of Twitter followers would definitely spread the word quickly.

"Not just me...a bunch of actors retweeted in support

of that poor assistant she railed on. No one wants to be associated with someone who treats people like that."

"Oh my God." The party is loud and cheerful behind us, but my mind is stuck processing the implications of what happened. "How did you know I was here?"

"The video that poor fan posted of the Wrath of Hillary P. is short, but I recognized the venue."

"Hillary will go mental because of this."

"But there will be no one to listen. No way will the network or her publishers support her after that. And I'm sure her products will lose market value. She's finished." He runs his warm hand through the loose hair by my face and kisses me on the nose. "Anyway, I thought we might have a glass of champagne. To celebrate."

"Celebrate Hillary self-destructing?" I ask as he escorts me into the back of his car and slips in beside me.

"Well, we should definitely make a toast to karma. But actually, I want to celebrate you."

"Me?"

"Yes. It's only been, what? A week? And already you're back on the red carpet? *Identity* magazine Instagrammed a picture of you touching up Liz Daniels during one of her interviews." I quickly pull out my phone and open up the app to see the image he's talking about on the *Identity* timeline. The caption reads "An #everydayhero looking after our own @LizDanielsEIC—thanks, Alex!"

I can't believe my eyes. "They tagged me!"

"You're going to get tons of job offers from that. She looked sensational. You did a great job, Alex."

"Thanks." I look up at him. "I love it." And he knows I mean a lot of things in that moment, because the kiss is a passionate, perfect representation of who Billy Fox is. I am swept away by it, by him, and yet I know my feet are firmly on the ground.

EPILOGUE

November

Flipping back through the last six months of my Instagram timeline is like looking through pictures in *Travel + Leisure* magazine. Well, maybe not a lot of leisure time, but still. I have seen some of the most exotic, beautiful places around the world, thanks in large part to my incredible career as a freelance makeup artist for *Identity* magazine, among other major publications.

The epic beaches I've seen are outshined only by the remote, out-of-the-way places I've escaped to with Billy when we both just need a break. To clarify, I don't do his makeup.

"Which you know still annoys me," he says as I laugh and playfully push him away.

"Stop reading over my shoulder."

"How else will I know what you're writing about me?"

"You'll just have to wait and see. Like everyone

else...Aargh!" My iPad falls onto the blanket Billy laid out on the grass below us. I'm grateful he knows his way around, because on my own, I don't think I would ever be able to find my way out of this impossibly beautiful valley on the South Island of New Zealand.

He pulls me underneath him, careful to adjust our position so as not to disturb the plastic cups of local wine and the basket of cheese all laid out nearby.

"You did the last movie. Why won't you work on this one?"

"I only did *Lasting Dance* because Bailey needed me to, and because you were just directing it." I repeat what I've said at least ten times. "You know features aren't really my thing."

"Too much continuity?" he teases me. I hate all the organization and script breakdown work that comes with being key makeup on a film. Going with the feeling of the day is more my style, meaning photo shoots of models and actresses are just my speed.

"But you were so good at it. And you know you liked being on set with me. We had fun," he says, smoothing his hands over parts of my body that remind me of how much fun we had. I can't begin to express how proud I am of Billy, and what incredible talent he has. He's in just as much demand as a director now as he is as an actor. It's fun to watch him pore over scripts and to help him find passion projects to pursue.

"I'll tell you what—find that indie you keep talking about. Some ultra-low-budget passion project you really believe in. I'll sign on in a heartbeat."

"Really? Why would that be different?"

"Because then it would be your girlfriend believing in you, supporting your dream," I say simply. "Not just giving the paparazzi an opportunity to pass judgment every time I come out of your trailer."

"What about my wife supporting my dreams? And me wanting to make all her dreams come true, too." I look up at Billy, thrown off. He's not laughing now. He's got that look of pure concentration on his face, and it's directed right into my eyes. I hadn't noticed before, but he is holding something between us. I force myself to break our eye lock and look at the gorgeous diamond ring in his hand. I gasp deeply, air finally coming back into my lungs. And without really realizing it, I feel tears start to seep from my eyes.

"So?" he continues softly. "What do you say?"

"Yes!" I laugh and cry and kiss him all at the same time. "I say yes!"

ACKNOWLEDGMENTS

First, I really have to extend my appreciation to my incredible editor, Stacy Creamer. She challenged me and encouraged me on this project. She believed in me and pushed me to make the story better.

Matthew Elblonk, my fabulous lit agent who is such a great supporter and always has my back.

Carrie Simons, my publicist and friend. With Carrie, anything and everything is possible. She has the will and the way.

My outstanding team at UTA—Max Stubblefield, Jacob Fenton, and Ennis Kamcili—are always providing me with plenty of fodder for these tales. Barbara Rubin is a remarkably skilled lawyer and confidante. I'm lucky to have her look after me.

I could never have written about New York City without my friend Stephanie. Thanks for helping me bring it to life in this novel—and fact-checking for me! There are a lot of dear friends who make special appearances in this book—Deidre, Corina, Melissa, Kirsten, Kristian, you all are always in my heart and thoughts when I write.

I must thank all my amazing, loyal fans. You all have stuck with me throughout my career, and I so appreciate your daily tweets and posts of encouragement on social media.

My family has always been such an important part of my life. My two awesome brothers, my parents who set such a strong example for us kids of a strong work ethic, dedication, and always striving to be the best we can be.

My wonderful, supportive husband always has my back when I dive headlong into another project. My kids always get on board for my new novels. They write their own stories or poems next to me while I work. We trade off reading aloud what we're working on. They inspire me to keep dreaming big.

If you loved OPPORTUNITY KNOCKS, check out these other novels by Alison Sweeney

"An entertaining, back-stage glimpse at those who organize the lives of the Hollywood elite."
—Jodi Picoult, #1 *New York Times* bestselling author

"With a lovable heroine and industry gossip, [*Scared Scriptless*] goes behind the scenes and straight to the heart."
—*Kirkus Reviews*

Also available as ebooks